Sandalwood Soap and Other Stories

Sandalwood Soap and Other Stories

Perumal Murugan

Translated by
Kavitha Muralidharan

JUGGERNAUT BOOKS
C-I-128, First Floor, Sangam Vihar, Near Holi Chowk,
New Delhi 110080, India

First published by Juggernaut Books 2023

With the exception of 'Loser', 'The Last Sacrifice' and 'Meowdi', the stories in this collection were originally published in Tamil in book form by Kalachuvadu Publications in the following books: *Perumal Murugan Sirukathaigal* (2016) and *Maayam* (2020).

'Grant Us Pardon, Saami', 'Sandalwood Soap', 'Hail, Comrade PM!', 'Magamuni', 'The Last Cloth' and 'Neelaakka' first appeared in *Perumal Murugan Sirukathaigal* in 2016.

'The Game', 'The Obstinate One', 'Thigh', 'Dog', 'Hunger' and 'Anointing' first appeared in *Maayam* in 2020.

Copyright © Perumal Murugan 2023
English translation copyright © Kavitha Muralidharan 2023

10 9 8 7 6 5 4 3 2 1

P-ISBN: 9789353451820
E-ISBN: 9789353451837

This is a work of fiction. Any resemblance to persons, living or dead, or to actual incidents is purely coincidental.

All rights reserved. No part of this publication may be reproduced, transmitted, or stored in a retrieval system in any form or by any means without the written permission of the publisher.

Typeset in Adobe Caslon Pro by R. Ajith Kumar, Noida

Printed at Replika Press Pvt. Ltd.

Contents

Introduction — 1

1. Loser — 7
2. The Last Sacrifice — 21
3. Thigh — 43
4. Anointing — 53
5. Meowdi — 63
6. Grant Us Pardon, Saami — 73
7. The Game — 89
8. The Obstinate One — 97
9. Dog — 113
10. Hunger — 127
11. Sandalwood Soap — 137
12. Hail, Comrade PM! — 151
13. Magamuni — 167
14. The Last Cloth — 179
15. Neelaakka — 191

Acknowledgements — 201

Introduction

There are worlds that you are guilty of not knowing. And then there are the worlds of Perumal Murugan's stories.

As a journalist with over two decades of experience, I've been proud of the places my work has taken me to, the paths it has opened for me and the people I have ended up meeting on my journeys. From an obstinately silent woman at a refugee camp in Sri Lanka who took hours to utter a single word to meeting the victims of the Veerappan hunt who opened up to journalists only to show the other side of the victory of the state over dacoity: where has journalism not taken me.

Or so I thought.

None of these, or the many other reports that I had worked on, had prepared me for Murugan's 'Sandalwood Soap'. It is the tale of a young boy whose job is to knock on the doors of toilets in a mofussil bus stand: that is, to urge people occupying the toilets to emerge sooner and so manage the invariably long queues in such places. 'It is as if shit is stuck on my body,' he tells the story's narrator, pleading to be taken away. The narrator buys him a bar of soap instead.

Murugan cloaks both characters in anonymity. The young boy is as anonymous as any face we could pass in a public place. He never fully sheds his anonymity even when we learn that he is the son of a friend of the narrator's from his village. His identity is meant only for someone he knows and trusts enough. That is not the narrator, who is as anonymous as the 'we' in any public place. We don't have time to nurture guilt about the toilet-policing children with whom we cross paths every day. The weakest of our attempts are violently put down by the demands of everyday life.

The bluntness in Murugan's language sears your heart. It makes you wish he would wave a magic wand and transport the young boy to a different, better place. There's certainly magic in the story: a material, hard-edged kind. By the end, we see the boy catapulted to adulthood. He has acquired a certainty in his persona and learned to wield some power in the little, wretched space he occupies.

He is like all of Murugan's women and men. They revel in the ordinariness of life. They are content with who they are. They falter when faced with extraordinary circumstances. And often, they crumble.

In 'The Last Cloth', an old woman is so terrified at the prospect of wearing a blouse that it stuns her into a torpor she has never once experienced, even at her advanced age. Murugan starts the story with the dilemma of the woman's well-educated son, who is revolted by his mother's bare breasts. She has never worn a blouse, not even in her prime. But the son, to whom this likely did not matter when he was growing up, hates it on his return from his modern medical education in a city. It is an astonishing illustration of the predicament spread across the lives of two people from different generations and how their relationship is transformed when one of them persists with a practice that has become obsolete for the other. In 'The Game', which deals with the changing nuances of the relationship between father and son, our sympathies are once again challenged, though their direction is reversed in favour of the young.

Another stunner in this collection is 'Neelaakka' – a story about a woman whose life becomes a bitter response to a biting comment about the stains on her teeth. Even though Murugan is the story's author, he treads carefully into the intimate world Neelaakka has created for herself, to escape the harsher one that exists outside. With delicacy, he lays bare to the reader her deliberate choice to wear herself down to her lowest point.

But for every Neelaakka, there's a Ramya. In 'Dog', Ramya stands up for herself and places her self-respect before her relationship with a man who won't stick up for her. Again and again, Murugan's women put up simple yet striking acts of rebellion – like the wife in 'Anointing' who throws her money at her bridegroom, or the one in 'Hunger' who refuses to sleep with her husband after his embarrassingly elaborate attempts to get her to go to bed with him. Tomorrow these women might go back to live their mundane lives, but today they have rebelled.

Murugan's writing offers deep immersion into the lives of people of his region but without any embellishment. There are people who would consider the deity Karuppasuran as one of their own and mourn his leaving, and then there is a woman like Velaatha who finds an uneasy and newfound respect among her colleagues and employer thanks to a local deity that possesses her.

Murugan navigates the complexities of varied relationships, through changing times and growing gaps, without making any compromise. In doing so, he also documents the changing façade of the rural life of the Kongu belt. In a remarkable feat, he creates vivid, dramatic stories that are rarely resolved with definite endings,

Introduction

happy or tragic. Often, the endings are just another page to turn. They are meant to merely show a new dimension to something that already existed – a relationship, an incident, a slice of life. The dimension turns out to be a huge revelation signifying a generational shift, or breaking a long-held faith: a change the region is perhaps not prepared for and yet is forced to accept. The disarming honesty and directness with which these stories are told are sometimes almost too difficult to handle – both as a reader and as a translator.

Translating Murugan is a very humbling exercise. It shows you the vulnerabilities and resilience of women and men in a world, the existence of which you were not aware. To dwell in that world twice – once as a reader and again as a translator – is an intense experience.

To get into the soul of a story like 'Sandalwood Soap', even as a reader, is an arduous task. It is difficult to dwell in the world of the young boy, even if only for a few pages, without shedding a tear or two, or without having your sense of judgement clouded by the behaviour of Murugan's characters. I couldn't translate it in one go: I had to take a break before I finished. I am haunted by Neelaakka, by the wreck she had brought upon herself, and by the dignity her author bestows on her by refusing to grant her easy pity or sympathy.

But the biggest challenge in translating Murugan is his dialect. He employs the distinct Kongu dialect in his stories which is not just difficult but almost impossible to translate. People who only read in English will have to miss out on this rich flavour of Murugan's original writing. But as he says, some things are lost in translation and some gained.

I do hope the stories that follow will help readers gain some insights into the life that Murugan wishes to represent in his brilliant oeuvre.

Kavitha Muralidharan

Loser

Kumarasuran realized that he understood what Kluze was saying only during a midnight phone call. It had been a day filled with office-related apprehensions. He had had an early dinner, locked his bedroom door and gone to bed. He needed complete darkness to fall asleep, so he had drawn the curtains on the windows to prevent the street light from seeping in.

But the darkness was more frightening than ever before. The images it created wandered across the room. He got up abruptly and turned on the night lamp. It was not enough. So, he turned on the tube light. So much light would not let him sleep, nor rid him of his fears.

He lay on his back. He had no idea when he finally fell asleep.

He heard Kluze's call clearly, near his ear. It was not the usual scream. The words 'Food, food!' could be clearly heard in a shrill voice. *Was the cat talking?*

He looked at Kluze waiting by him on his cot. The cat's voice grew louder when he opened his eyes.

'Hungry?' he asked and stroked it.

'Yes,' Kluze said. It lay close to him and pushed its head into his hand. It must have been in the bedroom before he'd locked the door behind him. The room had an iron cupboard. Kluze lay on top of it from where it jumped on to the shelf and slept there. In a corner of the shelf, Kumarasuran had made a cat bed using an old pillow. If Kluze slept there, it couldn't be spotted. You might just about notice it if you stood in the opposite direction of the room and looked in. He was ashamed of himself for falling asleep without noticing the cat.

Kluze closed its eyes, enjoying his caresses. Then it looked at his face after a while and asked again. 'Food?'

The realization suddenly hit him. Kluze was speaking human language. No, it was screaming. 'Food!' it screamed and bobbed its head up and down.

'Food,' Kumarasuran said too, and the two sounded similar.

He had missed it in the chaos of the night. He hadn't fed the cat, nor checked its water bowl. He had unlocked the house, gone inside, done this and that, but not a sound had been heard from Kluze. It somehow sensed that Kumarasuran's body was trembling in fear.

Loser

The cat was an animal created by fear. Any small sound unfamiliar to its ears, and the cat would hide. It never appeared in front of guests. You would have a hard time just discovering where it was.

Somehow, Kluze always knew whether Kumarasuran's body was filled with joy or fatigue, whether he was filled with sorrow, if his anger had accumulated or his fears had been aggravated. It would act accordingly. On a day Kumarasuran brought happiness home, it would run to him, ask him to spread his lap and lie there. On a day he was fatigued, it would lie in a corner and yowl. If he was sad, it would curl up in a corner. On days of anger, it would lurk atop the shelf. If he was in fear, it would go into hiding.

Kumarasuran understood the emotions in Kluze's voice, too. He had lately become familiar not just with the mood of its cries, but also its words.

He was feeling fresh and reinvigorated after his nap, and the clarity in Kluze's words filled him with excitement. He rose.

'Kluze, darling, what do you want?' he asked even as he opened the door and stepped out.

'I need food, I need food,' it said and ran behind him. He went into the kitchen to prepare its food. The curd from the refrigerator was too cold: Kluze wouldn't touch it if it was that cold.

Kumarasuran boiled water and put the cold bowl on top of the lid. He put some rice in another bowl and added water. All that remained was the addition of a little dried ayirai fish and Kluze would devour it in no time. It was the only creature that ate dried fish with curd rice.

When it smelled the rice, Kluze readied its stomach. You cannot talk to a cat when it defecates. It won't defecate properly if it hears the slightest sound. Kumarasuran had piled up some sand on a concrete platform where Kluze could go. Kluze now dug through this sand, sat inside and did its job. It then kicked up the sand to cover the faeces. Kumarasuran watched with admiration as it covered it up completely. It always knew the quantity of stools it was going to pass and dug into the sand accordingly. From where had it learned that it should defecate before a meal? A gift by birth. It would rub its feet on the doormat and clean itself. 'We are so unclean before a cat,' Kumarasuran would often tell his friends.

When he added curd to the bowl, mixed in the dried fish and kneaded the rice with water, Kluze screamed: 'Food!' and came running.

'It's for you, of course. Eat it slowly,' he said.

'Thank you.' Kluze began eating the food. The sand covering the stools was now a mound. He gathered it with a dustpan and flushed it down the toilet.

Loser

It was easy to clean the cat's litter. The difficult part was collecting the sand for it. Kumarasuran would set aside time on weekends to collect it. He would ride a long way to the outskirts of the city on a bicycle, his favourite journey. He would pass through the crowd, the hustle and bustle, taking in the lush fields stretched out on either side of the bypass road, on which only the sound of vehicles could be heard. He would see sheep and cattle grazing and spot the occasional human. Dogs would run around, playing. He would tell himself that this was life: to live in harmony with sheep, cattle, dogs and cats.

Choosing a spot where the sand was red, he would dig out enough to fill half a sack, which lasted two weeks. Kumarasuran made sure there were always at least two sacks of sand in stock. Things would get difficult if it rained because Kluze could not defecate on moist sand. He'd unknowingly brought home wet soil once, early on, and Kluze had run around the platform screaming, refusing to dig the sand. It had probably been saying, 'How do I defecate on wet soil, you fool?' he now thought. He had not known the meaning of its screams at the time. The cat had probably learnt human words in all the days that had passed since. Or was it that he understood its language?

More than a year had passed since he'd found Kluze.

The day was also celebrated as its birthday. To get to work, Kumarasuran walked a short distance to the bus stop from where he caught the bus and rode five stops to his office. He came back the same way. One evening, he was walking back home from the bus stop when he heard a kitten's screams from the bushes on the roadside at the end of the street.

He peeped into the bushes hesitantly. It was a kitten, yet to open its eyes, screaming incessantly. He put out his hands and picked it up. The kitten clung to his hands with its claws and assumed that the warmth of his palm was its mother's lap.

His fingers felt like they were being tickled. A new mother might have felt the same. At that moment, he was enveloped in a feeling of nothing but warmth. He brought the kitten home.

He had an unopened syringe from when he had been sick and needed an injection. That came in handy. He filled the syringe with milk and fed it to the kitten, drop by drop. He smiled at the speed at which it sucked the milk into its small mouth.

He was the only inhabitant of a house that had a single bedroom, a small living room and a kitchen. He worried about whether the landlord, despite living elsewhere, would accept a cat being brought up in the house. He made peace by telling himself that he would be able to explain when the owner visited, or do something or the other to deal with the issue. He searched the internet about bringing up a cat and learnt a thing or two. He was the first thing the kitten saw when it opened its eyes. The kitten perceived that Kumarasuran was its mother and believed it too.

Kumarasuran never let Kluze out. Even when it was a baby, he brought a cage to lock it in. He left water and milk in the cage. When he came back in the evenings, half the milk would have been drunk and the other half spilled on the floor. The cat would piss and shit in the cage. It was a huge task to clean the cage. The cat could not be kept like this as it grew. So Kumarasuran covered the windows with mosquito nets and let Kluze walk the house freely. He poured sand over the concrete platform. Then he was content that he had made every possible arrangement. Kluze wouldn't let lizards or cockroaches on the wall. It hunted and ate them. Not even a little insect could enter the house.

Kluze understood Kumarasuran. Every day, it followed him around the house until he left for work. After he left, it would go to bed. In between, it would wake up to urinate and eat. To bed again. It slept until he came back home. It changed beds according to the vibrations of the sounds outside – of vehicles, of dogs' barks and of humans' loud conversations. In the evenings, when it heard him open the door, it would scream and run towards him. He would pick it up and hug it. 'Did I leave you alone, Kluze? Were you afraid?' he would ask every day. The cat would rub its face against his in response.

Kumarasuran gave up many things just for Kluze. He wouldn't go to parties with friends. He wouldn't go back to his village, and when he did, he left in the morning and returned by evening, just as if he were going to work. Kluze dictated his movements. He would talk to his office friends about Kluze and its upbringing. They would laugh at him and turn away. He remained at home on holidays and felt safe about it.

'You have turned into a cat too,' his friends said.

'It would be nice if I did,' he told them.

A new superior officer joined the office where Kumarasuran worked as a junior assistant, a job he had started after passing a government examination two years earlier. He had to prepare the files, send them to three or four senior clerks and then submit them to the officer. The previous holders of this position had not proved to be much of a problem. They had lightly reprimanded Kumarasuran sometimes. Sometimes, a harsh word or two had erupted. He was used to it.

Loser

The new officer was different. He was constantly rude and used cruel words. He would throw objects at Kumarasuran's face. His office seat turned into a burning pyre.

It seemed Kluze had begun to speak at the sight of Kumarasuran burdened with misery and sequestering himself. After the night it first spoke, asking for food, it spoke to him every day.

'What was the problem today?' it asked when he entered the house in the evening.

'Let it be, how does it matter if I tell you?' he said and left.

Kluze didn't give up. It sat down at the foot of his bed and asked: 'What's the problem?' It climbed on his stomach and asked, 'What is the problem?' It stood on the kitchen platform and asked, 'What is the problem?' It constantly asked the same question.

Unable to bear the pressure, he started to tell Kluze the story one evening. 'The dog, you know?' (Cats do not like dogs.) 'He's constantly barking. You know what he did today? I took a file to get it signed and kept waiting. I stood, waiting and waiting. He didn't even look at me. He spoke to others, went to the bathroom, drank water, drank coffee. I was still standing. Not for a minute or two. I stood for two whole hours. My feet swelled up.

'Only then did he ask me: "Loser, what do you want?" Does he have a problem with my face? My language? My colour? I am not sure what he doesn't like about me. He threw the file. Papers went flying across the room. I'd be answerable if even a single paper went missing. I ran after the papers and started to collect them. He sat on his chair, looking at me, the dog.'

His tears fell on Kluze as it looked up at his face from his lap. It climbed on to his chest, trembling, stretched out its foreleg and wiped away the tears. 'Do not cry.'

But he could not hold back his tears. He hugged Kluze tightly, cried some more and, collecting himself slowly, continued.

'I collected the papers and came back. He asked the woman on the seat next to mine to bring the file and signed it. He told her that "that loser" shouldn't come to his place again. How am I to know what I have done?'

It was as if sharing the story with Kluze unburdened him. It gently scrabbled at his numb feet with its claws, bringing life back into them. 'Let it be, don't keep thinking of it,' it comforted him with words.

He was surprised at Kluze's knowledge of so many words. He picked it up and caressed it. He ought to treat Kluze to chicken this Sunday, he thought.

Loser

Every evening, as soon as he entered the house, he started to talk. He would cry for a few minutes. Kluze would sometimes offer solace, sometimes make fun. However, he made it a habit to tell Kluze everything.

One day, he said: 'Today he asked me to pour coffee for him from the flask. That is not my job. He sent his assistant away, probably deliberately. I didn't know how to pour out his coffee, or how much sugar to add, or how much to pour, or how hot the coffee should be. Neither did he say anything about it. I was too afraid to ask him. My hands trembled. I just about managed to pour the coffee out for him and left. Apparently, the cup had to be covered with a coaster. I had no idea. He started screaming, "Loser! Loser! Don't you know to keep it covered? Are you doing this so a lizard will fall into the coffee and let me die after drinking it?"'

Kluze got interested in the story. 'What happened next?' it asked.

He didn't notice the interest. He continued. 'I brought the coaster and ran towards him, but by then, he was drinking the coffee. He gulped a mouthful like a cow. And immediately spat it out. It splashed on the table and on me too. Not on my face, thankfully. "Loser, what is this? Coffee or dreck?" he screamed. The guy at the coffee shop made the coffee, someone else brought it to the office. If he shouts at someone who merely poured the coffee and calls him a loser, what am I even to do? Tell me.'

Kluze, it seemed, found this incident particularly interesting. It jumped from his lap to his shoulder. It rubbed its body on the floor. It climbed the windows and tore the mosquito nets apart. Kumarasuran was not able to take its joy. He went inside the room and locked it.

Kluze scratched the door and knocked on it. 'The story was good today. I became a bit excited. Don't be angry, open the door,' it pleaded.

He opened the door after a long while, concerned about its hunger. The cat was a sorry sight. It scratched his feet and begged to be forgiven.

Every evening, Kluze stood by the door expecting him. The moment it heard the iron doors screeching, it welcomed him crying, 'Come, come!' He had to start narrating the day's story immediately. Upon hearing the story, Kluze would lift its forelegs and walk around the house on its hind legs as Kumarasuran looked on admiringly. It seemed like a dance. Kluze seemed to demonstrate a different kind of excitement every day. Its body stretched out. When standing on its hind legs, it was tall enough to reach Kumarasuran's waist.

Loser

The senior officer was on leave that day. The entire office was jubilant. Yet they spoke about how things were dull at the office. Everybody walked around smiling. They went to drink tea together. When Kumarasuran came home in the evening, it was after an uneventful day. When the iron doors screeched, Kluze started scratching about, making a noise. He opened the door swiftly.

'Come, come,' he said to Kluze and tried to hug it.

'Tell me,' Kluze said.

'What should I say? Nothing happened today.' His face was beaming bright.

Kluze looked at him intently. Then it screamed in rage: 'Loser! Loser! Tell me the story!'

The Last Sacrifice

Kumarasu couldn't quite figure out how to uproot and remove Karuppasurasamy. He asked everyone around for ideas, but no one had any.

Some bucked the question, saying, 'This is a divine matter.'

Some pretended to give it deep thought.

'The tongue that utters a ploy to uproot the god will rot,' some said and withdrew.

The hundred-year-olds, their shrunken bodies tied to cots, were not of much help either.

'How to send Karuppan away?' Kumarasu never tired of asking.

'Is it even possible to move Karuppan from the fields?' some anxious responses came.

Karuppasuran occupied the northern corner of the last field, seated under a thick khirni tree in the form of a well-rounded stone. He was timeless. He stood witness to rains, sun, snow, cold and more. The khirni tree's family multiplied in the same spot. What currently existed was different from the original tree, and no one could tell which generation of its offspring now stood there. The tree had grown sharply and had let its aerial roots spread. Insects lived in abundance on the scales of the trunks. Ants lined up and climbed all over it. As the flowers would start to emit their scent, beetles and flies swarming to the tree would raise constant screeching sounds. When the fruits would hang in clusters and the leaves would fall, the tree stood like a skeleton, evoking sympathy. The fruits would eventually ripen, then explode, the seeds scattering with little fluffs of cotton that looked like small chicks.

Karuppan saw everything, but stood still as a stone, as if He saw nothing.

These fields had been first cultivated by an ancestor of Kumarasu many generations before. He had cleared the bushes on a rough strip of land, tilled the soil and begun to farm. His heart desired more land still, yet only so much was possible to attain. For a family, though, this land was more than sufficient. It was that ancestor who had discovered a round stone in the fields when ploughing. He had washed the stone and placed it in the northern corner of the fields, beneath a new khirni tree, on a small mound made of sand. That's how Karuppan became the guardian angel of the field.

When the British came to rule over the land of the demons, the lands were surveyed and taxed. Kumarasu's ancestors became its official owners. As of this writing, it was thirty-five acres of land.

It was Karuppan's duty to protect the field. When the winds howled in anger to destroy the crops, He would slow them down and turn them into a breeze. When it rained and water overflowed from the wells, leaving the roots to rot, He would break the furrows and let the water out. When the crops needed to grow, He would breed insects and worms. If the insects multiplied and began to destroy the crops, He would summon the birds. Spear in hand, he would drive away the pigs digging for groundnuts. He would set off a pack of dogs to drive away the jackals that came looking for a bite out of the throats of the lambs. He would protect the cows and give herbs to cure the rare diseases they contracted. Karuppan had endless jobs.

For all that he did, Karuppan was offered only three pujas a year. He was offered a sacrificial chicken in the first puja, a goat in the second and a pig in the third. It was only on puja days that the shrub around the khirni tree would be cleared. The round stone was washed with water. Flowers and sandalwood paste adorned the stone. A new lamp was lit, to cast more light – a large lamp, which, if filled with castor oil and lit with a thin wick, would keep burning till the next day. Figurines of a dog, a goat, a cow or a child – one or two – would join Karuppan for company, by way of fulfilling the vows of the people living on the fields. As they made pongal on each of the three feast days, they came up with prayers seeking Karuppan's blessings 'to help them continue the offering of pongal every year'.

Deaths followed births and the span of generations lengthened. The family grew, became a clan and set many cornerstones amidst the fields. Vehicle tracks, paths through shrubbery and pavements all ran alongside one another. The land was divided over and over, and eventually Kumarasu got two acres as his share. When dividing the land with his younger brother, Kumarasu got the part inhabited by Karuppasuran.

'What will we do with an angry god? Can we even give Him what He wants? We will take the other part,' Kumarasu's wife Mangasuri said.

Kumarasu was large-hearted at the time. 'Isn't it good if the god is on our side? It's a rare privilege. Karuppasuran wants to be on our side. Leave it, let Him remain in his corner.'

Mangasuri wouldn't agree. There could be no yield in an area where Karuppan was present. The heat in His eyes, along with the warmth of the khirni tree's shadow, would suffuse the area and turn the region arid. A considerable allotment of land had to be made for Karuppasuran. Mangasuri demanded more land, equal to his share. 'Only in these parts do we witness a demand for land in lieu of that occupied by a god,' the mediators said.

Someone remarked that when a woman mediated, it created more problems – there would be no end to them. But Mangasuri was adamant. 'What option does a woman who is married to a naive man have? She must be smart or she will be cheated,' she answered the mediators. The place occupied by Karuppasuran was measured in the shape of a circle. An equivalent portion of land – about one cent – was given to Kumarasu.

The small patch beyond Karuppasuran's temple belonged to Kumarasu. Next to it was a barren well, now covered by the trees and plants that grew inside it. Owls and pigeons nested there. There might have been some water in the well now and then. The levels rose when it rained. The well and a few feet of land around it was declared common to both brothers.

The younger brother was angry that his elder brother had cheated him and got away with more land. The villagers' talk left him further incensed. 'Didn't your brother take away more land in God's name?' they would ask.

'Did I give it up for that dog? I gave it up for God. I have the right to offer pongal and sacrifice animals to Karuppan every year,' he would reply.

It had been a long time since the three ritual pujas had been offered to Karuppasurasamy. Once a year, a day after Maatu Pongal in the Tamil month of Thai, a festival would be held for Him. One puja was abandoned after it became a disgrace to consume pigs. That was when the wild boars disappeared and sewage-bred pigs arrived. When it became a costly affair to invite the relatives and offer them a feast of lamb, the second puja was abandoned.

Since the god demanded three pujas, there were no rites at all for some time, nor any offering of pongal. One generation passed thus. But Kumarasu's grandfather couldn't bear the family simply watching as pujas were performed for the other guardians of the village's lands, nor the sight of the khirni tree overgrown with shrubs. He consulted a fortune-teller and started saying that 'a single puja is enough, Karuppan has agreed to it'.

Since then, a single puja was performed every year and a chicken sacrificed. Relatives who owned a share of the family's over thirty acres would come to offer pongal to

Karuppan on that day. More than ten chickens would be offered in sacrifice. On some years, four or five relatives would come together, light a lamp in devotion and share the curry among themselves. It might be divided, but Karuppan was still the guardian for the entire land.

Relatives who were not on talking terms with Kumarasu would come to offer pongal, too. He wouldn't stop those who came to offer their prayers. The sight of stoves burning in the open field after the harvest, from a distance, made it look like the big house had been set on fire. 'However much they fight, the relatives come together for one day in a year,' the villagers told each other, with a tinge of jealousy.

'Demons will divide, and the god will unite,' the older people said.

After Kumarasu and his younger brother parted ways, the animosity escalated and they stopped talking to each other. First, there was a quarrel among the women, in the year when his brother's cow came untied at night, entered Kumarasu's maize field and destroyed it. The verbal altercation escalated to the point of blows. The day of Karuppasuran's puja arrived while tempers were still raging. When the younger brother's wife brought the customary pongal, Mangasuri spoke tauntingly to her. The younger brother's wife talked back.

'A devil has stepped into my field,' Mangasuri said, in the ensuing quarrel.

'Wouldn't the devil catch hold of us merely for looking at your face? Are you the devil, or am I?' the younger brother's wife shouted right back. Attempts to pacify them by relatives who had brought pongal were futile. Barbs flew thick and fast, and it soon turned into a fight among the men.

The brothers came to blows on a field where the roots of the maize stood like the adze after a harvest. Both were hurt in the fight. The light emanating from the full moon ran through the fields. The visiting relations intervened and separated them. The brothers were grunting like pigs.

'I have every right to come and worship the god!' the younger brother shouted.

'Bring the land deed,' Kumarasu demanded. 'Let us see if it has been mentioned so.'

The practice was documented nowhere. It was customary for any relative to come and offer pongal to Karuppasuran. In any case, despite all the divisions, no one had stopped another from making the offering before. Kumarasu's question made everyone realize that they were no longer in times when oral promises held good.

The younger brother and his wife left without offering pongal. 'Does the god live only under this khirni tree? All the fields are His bed, all spaces His hunting ground. We shall place him in our heart, offer fragrant pongal and sacrifice a chicken. A stone planted is God. An offering of flowers is a puja. Next year, a Karuppasuran will stand guard under a khirni tree in my field. All of you can bring your pongal there.' The younger brother's wife roared these words as she left.

Those who were already at loggerheads with Kumarasu left without offering pongal, too. 'He says this to his own brother. Won't he say the same thing to us one day?' they wondered. Neither Kumarasu nor Mangasuri stopped them when they lifted the pongal pots.

'He didn't even stop us,' they lamented. 'Couldn't he have said that the fight is between him and his brother and that we need not leave without offering our prayers? After all, this is about God.'

Some people offered pongal since they had come all the way, anyway.

Gradually, the pongal offerings and chicken sacrifice stopped altogether. 'This is a god that demands three pujas. We have to offer pongal thrice and make sacrifices thrice. Otherwise, we must give it up. Can we observe the rituals thrice now? We will do them when we can,' Kumarasu responded to those who enquired. It was, in a way, the explanation he gave himself.

In the absence of pongal and puja, the khirni saplings sprouted on all four sides of Karuppasamy's mound. The bushes grew thick with thorns, making it impossible to cross his threshold.

Kumarasu's son Megasu was not inclined to farming. He said he wouldn't suffer the rest of his life with a handful of land, two oxen and four sheep. 'I can't be scratching at this land forever,' he said.

Four or five people pooled in some money to buy a borewell for their use. The borewells ran through the lands of demons and pierced through the earth. Those who didn't have the money sold their lands, invested their share and went into business. They could buy the land back whenever they earned enough money. Megasu insisted that their share of land be sold and that he wanted to go into business. Kumarasu did not want to sell. But no amount of cajoling would work with the son. Megasu attempted to consume pesticide when the arguments with his father reached boiling point. Then, Kumarasu agreed to sell the land. After all, his only son was more important.

Kumarasu's land fell in the panchayat area which started along the mud track that led to the end of the municipality's border. It could be sold off in separate plots. The cost of registration was higher within municipality limits and lower within the panchayat. There was only one mud road between the municipality and panchayat, and chances that the plots would sell like hot cakes were high.

Land brokers paid them repeated visits. Everyone liked the land, carved out of divisions. It lay in a rectangular shape, longitudinally, along the mud track: that meant a straight track in the middle and plots on either side. It was all very handy. But when they arrived at the last part of the land and got wind of Karuppasuran's presence, the brokers withdrew: 'He is a god of wrath. Remove him anyhow and then we shall proceed.'

When the brokers met Kumarasu next, they asked if Karuppan had been uprooted, with no clue themselves of how to uproot Him, or what to do with Him. 'Do it, somehow,' they told him.

'Let this land be allotted to the temple,' one broker suggested. 'In any case, when houses come up, people will come together and build a temple. You'll have to give up two cents, but that's fine.' It offered some hope.

The broker continued: 'Isn't this a vegetarian god?'

Kumarasu responded hesitantly. 'No, this is a non-vegetarian god. We've got to make sacrifices.'

'Then this won't work. The people who want to live in plots like these demand only vegetarian gods. An elephant god, even a cat god is fine. But a non-vegetarian god won't work. Find a way to remove it.'

Kumarasu had no other option but to seek ideas on how to do that. The astrologers he consulted said 'Ask me about installing a god, I will tell you. Don't come to me to remove it!' and chased him away.

He went in any direction he was pointed to, by anyone he came across. Nothing helped.

Disheartened, he thought of hiring a JCB machine to dispose of the idol. 'You call me to uproot God? Do you want me to die?' the driver of the machine shouted, livid when he found out. 'You wanted to blame me for this blasphemy and escape?'

Kumarasu managed to escape his wrath without getting beaten up. His son Megasu constantly drew a long face, as if he were about to pick up the pesticide at any moment and drink it down.

'Are you one to bother about your son? You think of giving it all up and handing over everything to your brother?' Mangasuri often shouted.

'I asked everyone what to do. Not one person knows. Why don't you tell me what to do with Karuppan? Let's see,' Kumarasu shouted back, irritated.

She was unfazed. 'Your grandfather met a soothsayer and said Karuppan didn't need three pujas, one would suffice. You claim to have been close to him, but you are not as intelligent as he was.' The casual remark was an eye-opener.

He remembered running around behind his grandfather as a child. His grandfather would take him along wherever he went. He took him often to a village called Aruvasuram. There was a middle-aged man in that village who used castor seeds for his soothsaying. Seated under a neem tree, clad only in a loincloth, the man would rattle seeds in his cupped palms, divide them half into each fist and put his hands down, one by one, to count in ones and twos. The predictions depended on how the numbers fell. The man would then clean up around himself and smear the neem tree with turmeric. Kumarasu used to play around the neem tree.

The fortune-teller would place a lamp as large as a pair of stretched-out palms beneath the neem tree. Before taking the castor seeds in his hands, he would fill the lamp with castor oil and light it. The image of his grandfather sitting in front of the soothsayer in all humility sprung up in Kumarasu's mind. The soothsayer never took money. He only ever accepted castor seeds. People would offer them to him in different sizes of bags and baskets and seek his guidance. If his words came true, people offered castor seeds in even bigger baskets.

It was unlikely that the soothsayer was still around. But there might be someone in his lineage: someone who was still telling fortunes.

One Tuesday morning, Kumarasu went to the village. The neem had grown taller and was magnificent now. Nothing else had changed. A young man, twenty or twenty-five years of age, was seated beneath the tree, seeking answers from the soothsayer. There were five or six people in the queue before Kumarasu. After their consultation, the people placed money under the neem tree, paid obeisance to the lamp and left. The amount of the fee was left to their choice.

Kumarasu put down his bag filled with castor seeds and looked around. This man might be the grandson of the soothsayer from his grandfather's time. Wasn't he too young, though? Would he be able to solve his problem? Kumarasu had his doubts. On the other hand, he had knocked on several doors. What was the harm in asking one more person, one who made predictions for so many people?

When Kumarasu's turn came, he explained his problem. The young man didn't say a word. He took the castor seeds in his hands, folded his palms in a prayer and opened them. Then he started counting the seeds. He did the same thing thrice.

Finally, he said: 'I asked Karuppasuran if He wanted to stay back or leave. "It is too hot and I cannot handle it. I will leave," Karuppan has said.'

Kumarasu was excited. Not one person until now had said he could remove Karuppan. He was hearing the words for the first time – from a boy.

How to remove the god? What was to be done? Who would lift the stone? Where could it be placed? Kumarasu asked the young man more and more questions. The young man's lips parted slightly. Captivated by that smile, Kumarasu stopped his questions and gazed into his face.

'Let's see,' the soothsayer said and took the castor seeds in his hands again, counting three times again.

Then he said: 'Karuppasuran said He wants to be thrown in cold water, to get rid of the heat. Offer fruits and flowers and sacrifice a chicken on a Tuesday. Pray to Him with all your heart. Then dig Him out, place Him in a small palanquin and bear it away along with your son. Carry Him out to the sound of drumbeats and send Him into the river. His body will cool down and He will happily stay there forever. No misfortune will befall you.'

Kumarasu had more questions, but the young man didn't give him the chance. He had to vacate the place for the next person. Kumarasu tucked a hundred-rupee note along with a bag of castor seeds under the tree and left, emboldened. Karuppan could be given a good send-off. He reached home and informed his wife and son. They were happy, too. Finally, the problem seemed to be coming to an end.

Then Mangasuri thought it over and said after a while: 'It will cost about a lakh.'

'One lakh?' Both father and son were taken aback.

She explained her calculation patiently. The river was twenty kilometres from the village. It would take about a day to walk to the river and return. At least ten drummers would have to accompany them. Even if they charged a nominal fee for beating the drums, they would ask more to walk the distance. A palanquin would have to be purchased: could Karuppan be carried out in an ordinary fashion? He ought to be wrapped in silk. Of course, there would be other things needed for the puja.

Even if father and son carried the palanquin, they needed at least four more people to walk with them. If they decided to invite their relatives, it wouldn't stop with just a few people. They would have to provide at least two meals that day to at least twenty to twenty-five persons. After sacrificing a chicken, they would have to serve chicken to their guests. A single chicken wouldn't be enough. They would need more chickens, perhaps a lamb. The feast would have to be ready by the time they got back from the river.

The expense would easily cross a lakh of rupees. They had saved up some money to get the son married. But if it were spent on Karuppan, they would be left without a penny. Many expenses remained to be incurred before the land could be sold and bring in money.

The courage instilled by the soothsayer now drained away. Kumarasu was fatigued. For about a week, no one in the house spoke to each other. They knew the way out of their problem but could do nothing about it.

It was summer. There was no crop on the land. When tending his sheep and cattle, Kumarasu often went to Karuppan. 'You are troubling us so much! Is this even fair?' he pleaded.

He couldn't stay idle. Seeking justice from Karuppan, he cleared the shrubbery from around the mound. Karuppan became clearly visible in the single blunt stone, as if He had folded both hands along the root of the khirni tree. Kumarasu couldn't stand the sight.

'A god ought to show the way, not obstruct it,' he said, his eyes welling up. He looked around to see if anyone else was there, and then cried his heart out. The dog that roamed about with the goats came to him and buried its head in his lap.

'The god doesn't love me as much as you do.' He hugged the dog and cried more.

Kumarasu usually lay on a cot in the goat shed. It was a Tuesday. Tuesdays arrived every week, but he couldn't do anything about it. He was unable to sleep. There were shadows lurking by the door, and he could hear whispers too. Wondering if a goat thief had come in, he slowly got up and came out. There were three figures. In the moonlight, he could recognize Megasu.

Seeing his father, the son said, 'We are going to take Karuppan out. If you want to come along, don't utter a word. If not, lie back down.' No one had known what he had been up to. He had brought two of his friends with him. *All we need, somehow, is a breakthrough*, Kumarasu thought.

Megasu had a rooster tucked in his arms. Another fellow had a basket on his head and a bag in his hand. The third carried one water pot on his shoulder and another by hand. Kumarasu gained confidence from their plans. He abided by his son's words and walked behind them without uttering a word. Mangasuri, sleeping inside the house, didn't wake up.

The boys worked fast in the moonlight. Kumarasu, who didn't know what to do, merely looked on. They bathed Karuppasuran and performed a puja with fruits and flowers. They opened a small bottle and sprayed the liquid all over Karuppan. The wind picked up the smell of alcohol. Karuppan would now listen to whatever they said. He wouldn't stop them no matter what they did. Megasu bowed in front of Karuppan. Awed by his knowledge of these things, Kumarasu did the same.

As soon as holy water was sprinkled on the rooster, it shook and flapped its head. Kumarasu was content. 'Karuppa, this is the last sacrifice for You,' he bellowed. 'You gave us your consent immediately. We are happy.'

The blood of the sacrifice flowed all over Karuppasuran. The chicken's wings were plucked and cleaned. Off to the side, a stove was lit. Megasu asked his father, who was standing idle, to chop up the chicken.

As the curry cooked, the boys opened another bag and took liquor bottles out. Were they drinking using Karuppasuran as an excuse? Kumarasu was livid but couldn't express it. Megasu sat with his back to his father. He had ordered him 'not to speak'. If Kumarasu violated the order, Megasu would shout in anger. Gone were the days when the son was afraid of the father. Today, the father trembled in front of the son.

The three young men sat together. Would they give him some curry or not? Confused, Kumarasu sat next to the stove and stirred the curry with a ladle. Then he took a piece and put it in his mouth. The chicken sacrificed for Karuppan should not have tasted good: Karuppan should have sucked the essence and spat out the dregs. Nonetheless, this tasted good. It needed to stew more.

Holding out a plastic tumbler that could be crushed merely by taking it in hand, Megasu's friend asked: 'Is the curry ready, Uncle?' Kumarasu's expression made it clear he did not approve of drinking with young boys. He paused a little while before taking the tumbler. He put the curry on an areca plate before it had finished cooking and took it for himself.

Kumarasu finished off the drink without lifting his mouth from the tumbler. He ate two pieces of chicken. The men spoke among themselves while eating. They kept pouring him liquor. Parottas came. He didn't know how much he drank and how many parottas he ate.

When his head started spinning and he wanted to lie down, he could see Megasu and his friends getting up. Stumbling, Kumarasu got up too. The clouds covered the moon. There appeared to have been a little altercation between Megasu and his friends on who would lift Karuppan out of the soil.

'I will lift Him. I have seen everything in life. All the misfortunes that Karuppan brings, let them end with me,' Kumarasu spluttered.

The young men remained silent.

One of Megasu's friends took Kumarasu by the hand. Another one switched the torch on in his mobile phone. A third removed the flowers that covered Karuppan.

'Saami!' Kumarasu cried, folding his hands, and hit the side of the stone with a wooden stick. The stone was uprooted in a single blow. Kumarasu pulled it out of the ground.

'This isn't even an arm's length. Did we struggle so much for this stone?' one of the young men said.

Megasu took the stone out of Kumarasu's hands and placed it in the basket. He strew flowers all over it. He opened a bottle of liquor and put it inside. Then he lifted the basket. A friend played auspicious music on his mobile phone. The procession of Karuppasamy accompanied by drumbeats lasted about a hundred feet. Then Megasu threw the basket into the barren well. The sound of Karuppasuran falling into the water and becoming one with it could be heard clearly. Some birds flew out, screaming. A lamp, broken figurines and other items went into the well one after another.

Kumarasu walked unsteadily towards the well. 'Saami, we are not sending You off anywhere,' he said. 'This is the place where You have dwelled. This is the earth You ruled. Stay here, in the coolness, forever, and protect us,' and prostrated in front of the well. The drumbeats stopped.

Thigh

Murugesh hadn't been to work in ten days. He wasn't sure how long it would take to resume work. He had applied fomentation and poured hot water on the thing, as his mother had suggested. He shied away from showing it to her when she demanded to see it, ashamed of lifting his dhoti and exposing his thigh. 'Hey, isn't this the same hand that held your weenie, caressed and washed it?' His mother laughed. 'Look at you, refusing to show your thigh to me now.'

How could he expose the swelling on his thigh? It was round and thick, hardened like a cyst. He felt better only after taking a painkiller injection. If he had neglected it for a few days longer, the doctor had said, he might have had to go under the knife. His younger brother, who had taken him to the doctor, had probed him about the growth. He hadn't been willing to believe the story that Murugesh told everyone – that it was indeed a cyst. Murugesh had even asked his brother to leave the room when meeting the doctor.

It's hard to hide anything these days. He couldn't even hide his thigh.

Worse than losing out on his wages if he skipped work, he was very worried about not meeting her. He considered walking slowly, taking the minibus she took, meeting her and returning on the same bus. But he couldn't put on trousers. It was difficult to even move his leg. She didn't have a mobile phone. Her family refused to buy her one. He had offered to buy one for her, but she had refused. It was difficult to hide it at her home. She didn't want to be on edge always, she had said.

What would she think of his disappearance? She would have hopefully realized he was ill, prayed for his recovery and return but been left disappointed. He was hesitant to send her a message through someone. Who could he ask? Would they convey the message properly? What if they teased her and offended her? At work, he had said nothing more than that he was unwell as a reason for going on leave. His colleagues would all turn up together if they knew the actual reason. He would have to explain everything to them. Then they would chide her and Shankar. Everybody would come to know of it.

Thigh

Shankar was yet to visit him, even though he was from the same village.

Shankar lived on the fields on the border of the village, where his parents had taken a piece of land on lease to farm. Murugesh lived within the village. Shankar, knowing the reason Murugesh was on leave, had likely avoided coming to see him. That was good. Murugesh wondered if her attention would turn to someone else in his absence. But he pushed the thought away forcibly and filled his heart with hopes of being with her. Would she have known from the conversations of the village youth in the minibus? Wouldn't someone have asked where he was and someone else responded that he was unwell? She would have been all ears for conversations about him.

He couldn't be at peace, however hard he tried. This pain was greater than the one in his thigh. He thought constantly of ways to communicate the reason for his absence to her. None fit the bill. He realized now that he should have gotten hold of the supermarket's phone number. She wouldn't talk to anyone. Even to him, she would speak only during their commute on the minibus. She hardly looked at his face during these conversations. She wouldn't go anywhere with him either.

She worked at the supermarket. Her house, the supermarket and the minibus were the only places she was acquainted with. 'Are you such a good girl?' he would tease her.

'And look at the bad man this good girl is talking to,' she would say.

He had done some thinking to come up with an idea to keep talking to her. She had to walk a bit from the bus stop to the supermarket and back. He began to join her when she walked that small distance. He would disembark at the bus stop and wait for her. She would come and they would walk together. He would stop when the supermarket was a hundred feet away. She would go into the supermarket without looking back. He would stand and continue to look at her for some time.

It was the same in the evening. After work, he would go stand a hundred feet away from the supermarket. She would come and they would walk to the bus stop together. He would walk slowly to savour the conversation. He wanted to walk with her for long distances, but it lasted only a few moments. He would end the walk with a sigh. Before reaching the bus stop, they would separate, then board the same minibus.

Just once, he'd bought her bhelpuri from a popular street stall in town. She couldn't relish it fully. She kept looking around, worried that she was going to be caught. After that, she refused to go there. He learnt that she liked bhelpuri.

Thigh

He found a way out. He started to get bhelpuri packed for her when they met. She would put it in her bag. The bus proceeded towards her town after a sizeable crowd got off at his. She would eat the bhelpuri after that.

She was very secretive about their relationship. But people were sharp enough to recognize even the slightest of romantic gestures. Obviously, everyone knew about them. But nobody had a problem with it. As long as their families didn't know, they didn't have a problem either.

The problem, however, arrived in the form of Murugesh's friend Shankar.

Both were construction painters. They worked for an agent, one who hired more than ten persons. The agent's job was to find assignments for the workers. He did not send all of them to a single place. He had contracts to paint at least three buildings at a time. This agent would go to buildings where the painters couldn't mix the paint. He would mix the paint for them and teach them how to do it before he considered his job done.

In these buildings, the main doors, made of teak, needed polishing. The polish shone like flowing ghee. This mixture was the one secret that the agent refused to teach to anyone. It was a secret that only he knew. For teak doors alone, he would do the job by himself.

Murugesh had learned his work from this agent.

He had joined him after tenth standard. It was now his seventh year at work, and the agent considered him trustworthy. But not even to him would the agent disclose the secret of the polish. 'Wait a bit longer,' he would say, if Murugesh confronted him. 'I will teach you later. If I teach you now, you will gather four people and emerge as my competitor.'

He used to try to steal a glance when the agent made the mixture, but it was no use. The agent would look like he was preoccupied, chatting with someone, yet the mixture would be ready in a flash. Murugesh wondered if the agent knew some kind of jugglery. Sometimes he threatened the agent by saying he would get work elsewhere, but the agent appeased him one way or another every time.

If only he could learn that mixing, Murugesh thought, he could work on his own.

Shankar was not interested in these nuances and didn't care for the niceties of painting. He would tell Murugesh to learn the art and start out on his own. 'I will be the first person to join you.' Shankar was two years older than Murugesh.

It was Shankar who spotted her on the minibus. He did not speak a word to her, nor went anywhere near her. He never took his eyes off her until she got out. If she glanced at him by accident, Shankar lowered his eyes and hung his head down.

Thigh

He would say that he had installed her in his heart and built a temple there for her. But if asked to talk to her, he hesitated. 'A time will come,' he would say.

'Someone else will do it before you,' Murugesh would tease him. That it turned out to be Murugesh was an irony of sorts.

She looked like a wall painted in pale yellow. Green nerves ran through her hands. She wore bindis of different colours, ones that suited her face. She wore jasmine flowers every day. The dark tresses that fell to her waist were in striking contrast to the white jasmine. Her clothes accentuated her skin tone. She had only three handbags, but she always carried the one that matched with her outfit.

Shankar's love was unrequited, but everyone on the minibus, from the driver and conductor to the students, had a thing for her. Some thought they had won her over and struck up conversations. She would reply too but wouldn't speak more than three words. Since the minibus's route started in her town, she would find a window seat, and hardly look around. One day she would sit on the right and another day on the left. If she sat on the right in the morning, she would sit on the left in the evening.

Like everyone, Murugesh was excited to see her. But because of Shankar's efforts, he couldn't do much. Shankar used to keep count of her outfits and knew how many she had. They called him a fool. Everyone knew that Shankar couldn't bring himself to talk to her, nor was she destined for him. Only Shankar remained unaware of this.

Then, unexpectedly, Murugesh encountered her in private. He had once gone to the supermarket to buy something and realized that she was working there. Surprised, he had asked her: 'Don't you travel by Aarthi Minibus?'

'How do you know?' she asked. The gentle smell of her voice embraced him.

'Everybody who takes the bus knows you.' He had smiled. The smile communicated how special she was. She smiled back and blushed. He didn't want to continue the conversation; it wouldn't augur well for his self-respect. The next day on the minibus she smiled at him lightly and turned away. When everyone imagined the smile was intended for them, Murugesh knew well that it was for himself.

Every day after that, Murugesh was welcomed with the same small smile. She would smile when he boarded the bus, looking at him through the window. She changed her habits and started sitting on the left, just to be able to do so. He went to the supermarket once or twice, making it look unplanned. He took pains to look good on those occasions.

Thigh

On the day that he styled his hair after a favourite actor of his, her smile was slightly wider. She even made an appreciative gesture and called it nice. It was as sweet to him as being kissed. He stood mesmerized.

That was the day that others got wind of it, it appeared.

After that he had met her again when he visited her town to see a performance at a temple festival. He couldn't focus on the dancers and kept looking at her. She did the same. The next day, the festival featured a play. Even though it was not his favourite kind of performance, even when his friends refused to accompany him, he went, taking his grandfather along on a two-wheeler because he had wanted to see the play. She had come too, just as he had expected. On that day, he confessed his love and obtained her approval. It was evident to everyone that she liked him.

Shankar didn't talk to him for a few days. Murugesh was worried about how to respond if Shankar confronted him about it. For how long could he avoid Shankar? The agent paid them both every Saturday. He had just taken a big painting contract. Since it required the cooperation of all his workers, he had arranged a feast for them on wage day. He took all ten of them to the TASMAC bar outside the village, told them they could drink and eat whatever they liked, and joined them himself.

Murugesh occasionally drank a beer. It came free that day, so he decided to have two. He didn't see what Shankar was drinking. Each person sat with the people they were comfortable with. The bar was full because it was salary day. Many had left, but the painters were still hanging around. Murugan gave Murugesh company in drinking beer. They drank two beers and urinated thrice. They discussed buying one more beer and sharing it.

Shankar came looking for him, befuddled.

'Motherfucker, you somehow managed to impress her. Be blessed,' he said, and closed his fist and landed a firm punch on Murugesh's right thigh.

The punch felt like a rock. Despite the intoxication of the beer, Murugesh felt the pain. Yet, he decided not to express it. 'I am sorry, da,' he told Shankar, rubbing his thigh.

'Stay blessed, da,' Shankar said again and raised his hand to land another blow. This time, Murugesh took his leg in. When he left after finishing another half-bottle of beer, he felt a numbness on his thigh. He staggered all the way home.

The next day, his thigh had a blood clot and was swollen. He couldn't move it.

Anointing

Murugesh had been married for a month. Just as he was taking a breather after all the wedding-related rituals and temple visits, relatives started to invite him and his wife for customary feasts. He would visit one of these relations for a feast every weekend. The relatives called the practice vaichu kodukirathu – gifts to keep. They would invite the newlyweds to a lavish spread. Then they would place money on betel nuts and hand it over to them. The bride and the groom were to pay their respects and receive the money. This enabled the extended family and the new couple to get acquainted with each other and helped the newlyweds out with some quick money.

Murugesh worked as a clerk in the panchayat office on a daily wage basis. He was a graduate. To study further, he would have to relocate. But he couldn't expect his family to bear the expense, nor was he keen to spend so much on his studies. That money, saved and deposited in a bank, would at least earn him some interest, he thought. So he looked for any work he could get in the village while he prepared for the government's competitive examinations.

There was no competitive exam he hadn't taken in the last three years. He just hadn't cracked any of them. He always lost out by a mark or two.

Certain major cities had training centres for such exams. But they demanded big money for coaching. He borrowed lecture notes from those who went to these centres and tried to study them. Nothing worked.

Murugesh's father ran a small grocery store in a room made from cardboard sheets, on a vacant lot next to the bus stop. The job offer at the panchayat office came just when Murugesh had been wondering if he too ought to settle for a life supported by the grocery store.

The panchayat president, a relative, had helped out. But the job wouldn't become permanently his just like that. There was a process which would start only after the government sent a directive making it permanent. Murugesh would secure a confirmation if he were willing to spend a few lakhs. He was confident of raising some money when the time came.

Anointing

The panchayat office was two miles from his village. He spent nothing on transport and could come home for lunch. The salary was, of course, low. But he had opportunities to make a quick buck. He didn't even have to demand anything. People would offer him a fifty or a hundred for small errands. All he had to do was accept whatever was given. People were accustomed to such practices. Tallied together, these earnings were enough to run a family in the village.

But still, it was difficult to find a bride for him with his present job status. 'Is it a permanent job?' The question left him stumped. He tried, in various ways, to tell people that it would soon become permanent. No one took him seriously.

The girl's father shared in his hope, though, and agreed to get his daughter married to him. The man had two daughters and a son. He had given his eldest daughter away to a family that lived far from the household. That family was better off than their own. The daughter couldn't visit her birth family frequently nor could they visit her. Even if they did, the groom's family indirectly mocked them for their financial status. The father-in-law decided his second daughter wouldn't meet the same fate. He set two conditions when looking for a groom for her.

The groom's family had to live in the vicinity, and they could not be better off than his own. Murugesh seemed like an appropriate candidate.

The bride was educated only until the twelfth class. The groom was a college graduate. The father-in-law thought the job would become permanent. All he had to do was offer a little financial help at the right time, and his son-in-law would rise to the occasion. He believed that this son-in-law would be grateful for the assistance, and that he would treat his daughter well.

Murugesh was happy to get not just a bride, but also the promise of money. He was extremely respectful towards his father-in-law. In typical bridegroom fashion, and hoping to rise in his father-in-law's estimation of him, he remained obsessed with his wife.

The couple got invited to keep gift feasts from both sides of the family. They were careful not to let this create trouble between them and planned, accordingly, to accept invitations from each side. Murugesh was particularly proud when he took his wife to these feasts on a two-wheeler, dressed impeccably, with flowers adorning her hair. He felt as if the village were talking about how compatible they were. He imagined the young men his age brimming with jealousy and smiled at them with pride.

Anointing

On the first Saturday after their wedding, they went to the house of her eldest aunt, her periyamma. There were many favourite dishes of his at lunch. He devoured the meal, while his bride ate gently and slowly. He finished before she did and waited. When she finally noticed him, it appeared to her that he was getting impatient with her, and that the other women were laughing at her for making the husband wait. She wrapped the banana leaf and got up.

'Couldn't you eat slowly? Will you even digest your meal if you eat so fast?' she asked him when they got a minute alone washing their hands. He didn't know how to respond and simply grinned at her.

After the meal, Periyamma handed over the betel nut plate. He fell at her feet before accepting it. It was difficult to prostrate after the meal. He put the betel nut to one side, took the five-hundred-rupee note on the plate, and put it in his pocket. 'Isn't he clever?' someone remarked and others laughed.

He lowered his head, embarrassed that he hadn't held the betel nut for a bit longer. He wondered what his wife would think of him. When he raised his head, the plate was being offered to her. It appeared that she had been given two notes. They had probably given them the same amount in different denominations. Perhaps, as the house was her aunt's, she had been given more money.

After a nap, they left to go home. While driving back, he wondered if he should ask her about the money but decided against it. Wasn't the humiliation over the betel nut enough for the day? What would she think of him? She would give him that money anyhow, he thought. But she did not give him the money that day, nor the next. They did not talk about it at all.

It was her money. What did it matter? The money was meant for the family. So he told himself. To his mother, who asked about the money, he retorted: 'Am I going there for the money?'

'Each of you doing your own thing,' his mother said and had more to add. He shut his mother up. The wife observed the conversation between mother and son, yet she neither spoke of the money she received nor gave it.

The following weekend, they went to another round of feasts. On Saturday, they went to his athai's house. He felt that she was given more there too. Why would his own aunt do that? Did she want to show off to the new bride?

A month and a half after they had been married, Murugesh was still hesitant to talk openly with his wife. He needed to be more careful in money-related matters,

Anointing

but he believed he had already cut a sorry figure that first week and decided to be silent.

Over the next two weeks, there were more feasts. Everywhere, he was given a single five-hundred-rupee note. He noticed that she was given more than one note. Before he could figure out the amount by the colour of the note, she had tucked it in. She appeared unaware of his attempts to find out how much she had received. Murugesh imagined that she would have saved more than five thousand rupees at this point. What would she do with it? Would she give it to her father? Or buy saris for herself?

The next time they went to a feast, he couldn't contain his curiosity. It appeared once again that their hosts gave her two or three notes. He came up with an idea.

He drove to a petrol pump for fuel. She alighted from the bike and stood in a corner. He stayed in his seat and opened the lid of the tank. His plan was to pretend that he couldn't reach for the wallet in his back pocket. When the tank was filled, he started the engine.

'Give me two hundred rupees,' he said to her in a raised voice. 'I cannot reach my wallet, I'll give it back later.'

He made it sound casual. But it was evident that she

didn't like his demand. Annoyed, she asked, 'Can't you climb off and get it? What's the hurry?'

He felt humiliated that she spoke to him so in front of the petrol pump man. They didn't speak to each other the rest of the way home.

As he changed his clothes in their room, he saw her searching her own cupboard. He wanted to ask her about it but didn't. He put on a lungi and got into bed. He wondered how to initiate a conversation, how to make peace with her. She was taking things out of the cupboard and leaving them outside. He tried to guess every sound – the cupboard door opening, closing, the rattle of the locker inside the cupboard – and figure out what she was up to.

He was lying with his back turned to her. He could hear the screeching sounds of doors moving and saris being picked out. *Did I make a mistake by asking for money at the petrol pump? he wondered. Didn't I tell her I would give it back? Why would she do this now?*

His thoughts came in a chain. Maybe it had been a mistake to have said that he would return the money. He wondered if it was possible to kiss and make up. He was worried at the thought of her leaving for her father's place.

'Look here,' she called. He couldn't comprehend it at first. 'Look here,' she said firmly and loudly. He was

Anointing

shocked that she was addressing him in casual speech for the first time.

She picked a stack of notes out of her sari and threw it at him. 'Here, catch! You demon! Here they are, take them!' she screamed, enraged and frenzied. It was as if his body had been anointed in hundred-rupee notes.

Meowdi

The cat caught their attention on a particularly idle day, when they were about to run out of conversation. It was not the same cat that had been wandering in and out of the house so far. It appeared like new life, washed in fresh light. It would turn its head and look when called, '*Meowdi!*' Fire shone in its eyes. Its cries were like the music of a violin. Their eyes and ears were rejuvenated.

Nobody had expected the Covid lockdown to stretch on like this. A few days, a couple of weeks: you could stay home, get some rest, catch up on all the movies you had left unwatched. Mangasuri was excited at the prospect of finally having sufficient time to spend nurturing the plants on her terrace, all lovingly purchased; at the opportunity to have relaxed conversations about things she had always wanted to talk about with her husband and daughter. But it did not turn out that way.

There were rumours that the virus was airborne. They closed the windows and stayed home. The groceries they had bought a day before the lockdown, in that mad rush, would last for another six months. Tomatoes and onions were, of course, an issue, but it was possible to cook without them.

They made sure that no one person breathed over the other.

The daughter, a schoolgirl, was content with her laptop and cell phone, almost always, in her room. Mangasuri worked as a teacher at a private school that held monthly examinations. She was often exasperated by the answer sheets. She had dreams of being suffocated in a pile of words. Covid gave her a major release from this situation. She celebrated it by making moong dal payasam.

The daughter laughed. 'The world's mourning, but we are eating sweets!'

'Do not overthink it; enjoy your payasam,' Mangasuri said.

'Wouldn't we be like the man in the old story who was told never to think of a monkey when taking his medicine, who ended up never taking the medicine because he invariably thought of a monkey every time?' her husband asked.

They laughed together. The lockdown had a beautiful start, indeed.

Meowdi

Mangasuri's husband was a clerk in a government office, one who had never been able to take a single day off and would even bring work home. She had thought he would be stressed by the lockdown. But he was not. He slept long hours. He took a nap after every meal. He appeared to be making up for all the sleep he had lost since birth! He would call various people on his cell phone and talk at the top of his voice. The daughter would come out of her room and chide him to speak softer. Then he would go take a walk on the terrace. This was how time passed for him.

Mangasuri was buried under housework. She had to do all the chores since the domestic worker couldn't make it. She constantly felt the house was dirty. Every day she cleaned one part of the house and tidied things up. The daughter and husband gave her different ideas on how to do it. She would arrange things after they arrived at a consensus. The living room now appeared spacious. They talked about beautifying it further. The daughter had expensive suggestions. Mangasuri let them pass.

She cooked breakfast and lunch in the morning, and kept the dinners light. The husband washed the dishes. They had long conversations during meals and into the night. The discussions were usually about their family relations on both sides. The biases, cheating and treachery of these relatives came to light. The couple had differences of opinion on these issues sometimes. They spoke in support of their own relatives and opposed the spouse's relatives. These conversations were not peaceful. One or the other would raise their voice. Sometimes, that would turn into screaming. Then, after some time, they would make peace with each other like none of it had happened. The daughter would emerge from her cave and complain about the tedium of their actions.

One evening, they went to the terrace. There were human faces on all the terraces. The moon had risen early that evening. Their usual conversations changed tack. Mangasuri spoke about school and her parents. He talked about his colleagues. The daughter, surprisingly, joined in. '*You* are happy, but look at me – I'm worried about the exams,' she said. She was about to give her final exam. Some confusion about these examinations ensued – whether they would be held and, if they would be, then in what format. The conversation then turned to comforting the daughter.

For some days, they kept going to the terrace. They could see all the houses on the street from there. They would gossip about the residents of the houses.

'Why are you angry on them?' the husband asked Mangasuri.

It was evident that he was trying to camouflage his ignorance about the neighbours in question.

She pointed to a terrace four houses away and asked: 'Tell me, who lives there?'

'Why should I care? Let it be any dog,' he said, and went, clattering down the stairs. She stayed on the terrace for a long while.

A certain impact was felt. They did not talk to each other. The daughter realized what was happening and spoke to them separately. She acted as a go-between, telling one what the other said. A huge silence enveloped the house in which only the daughter's voice was sometimes heard.

One day, when they were having lunch, with just the sound of the utensils clanking, Meowdi slowly walked in.

It stopped next to Mangasuri's chair and looked at her. Suddenly, it took a leap and landed on her lap. She smiled, her heart warmed, and spread her lap for the cat. She was proud that the cat chose her from among the three human beings there.

'I always pet you, but you go to Mother instead of coming to me?' the daughter asked. The cat was now curled up comfortably on her lap.

'Where have you been roaming around to get this tired?' Mangasuri asked the cat and caressed its head. It closed its eyes. The husband smiled a bit.

'Look, it demands the petting,' he started the conversation casually. She smiled back and said something in response. When the daughter left, she twitched the cat's ear.

'Jealous,' Mangasuri said.

'Wouldn't she be?' the husband asked.

The cat came to their house all on its own. It had been a kitten four or five months earlier when they had spotted it in their yard. The daughter had seen it first and brought it some milk. The cat was initially petrified, then smelled the milk and hesitantly tried it.

Mangasuri had been annoyed. 'Why this now?' she had asked.

'Poor thing, Amma,' the daughter had said. She had persuaded her mother. After that, the cat turned up often for milk. They could not be sure if it was male or female, but the daughter was certain that it was a female cat, and named it Meowdi.

Meowdi did not stop at the yard. It slowly made its way into the house. 'Look, how brazen it is!' Mangasuri would say but did not chase it away.

'If the cat sheds its hair, we might get asthma,' the husband said.

'We can clean it up,' the daughter replied.

'Will you?' Mangasuri asked her.

'Haven't I? I sweep the house every time the domestic worker doesn't show up,' the daughter said. She picked up Meowdi and caressed it. It got along with the daughter and did not fuss much.

'Who knows where it has been and what it eats?' the husband said.

'Hmm? Who can be as clean as a cat? It even covers its own shit. It cleans its paws and mouth after it eats. We take a bath once every four days. What can we even say about a cat's cleanliness?'

It was evident what she was referring to: he would not bathe on holidays. He didn't say a word after that. Meowdi was allowed to walk in and out of the house at any time. If it had to leave when the door was closed, it would let out a specific cry, and someone would open the door. The daughter created an additional path by cutting out a part of the mosquito netting on the windows.

With a cat in the house, the lizards hid themselves away. The rats were nowhere to be seen. The shrew mice changed places. The cockroaches, too, disappeared. Mangasuri fed the cat curd rice. When they cooked meat, she kept some pieces aside for it. She even bought dried fish from the market to give to the cat every now and then. She competed with the daughter in feeding it.

The cat was now part of the household. During the lockdown, it remained inside and slept in the loft in the daughter's room. It hardly stepped out, perhaps because there were humans in the house and there was no scarcity of food. Or perhaps it was afraid of the dogs now roaming on abandoned streets. The cat had vanished inside a cave, Mangasuri thought, just like her daughter.

From the day Meowdi leapt on to Mangasuri's lap, she felt an overwhelming love for the animal, and tended to it more carefully. When she was on the dining chair or on the sofa in the living room, the cat would crawl into her lap. It would not go to the daughter's lap despite her cajoling.

'You have no love for me,' said the upset daughter. The cat heard her voice, opened its eyes and merely looked at her. It seemed to have understood what she said.

Another time, when Mangasuri was busy in the kitchen, the daughter screamed: 'Amma! Amma, come and look here!' The cat was on the daughter's lap. She had never seen her so excited. She thought the cat might jump into her lap if she sat down, but she decided against it and moved away, merely expressing her surprise. The daughter remained seated until the cat left her lap. It sometimes sat on the husband's lap too.

It became a game between them and the cat. It would

come in when all three were around. They would call for the cat together: 'Meowdi!'

It would look at them, fake a leap in front of everyone and land suddenly on one lap. They would make a noise, excited. The cat, unable to tolerate the noise, would jump down. Then they would decide that they wouldn't make a noise if the cat did jump on somebody's lap.

The house was no longer silent. There was no fatigue on any face. Conversations began with Meowdi. The daughter spent more time outside her room now.

The cat's presence changed everything. Mangasuri chatted with the cat while cooking. The family spent time talking about the cat and looking forward to its visits. They were astounded by the beauty of how it jumped into a lap, the way it slept. They loved how it used its own paw as a headrest. It jumped into each person's lap at different times. When it chose one lap, the rest, in disappointment, would say, 'I will teach you a lesson when you come to me.'

They had just sat down to lunch on that day. The cat walked into the room. The three exchanged a secret smile. The husband was on one side of the table, while Mangasuri and the daughter sat facing him. The cat jumped into the husband's lap. He felt very proud. He caressed its head and spread his lap wider. The cat felt uncomfortable, for some reason, and jumped out to go to Mangasuri's lap.

'Won't you come to me?' the daughter crooned to it.

The husband's face turned red. 'You gestured to it to come to you,' he accused Mangasuri.

'When did I ever? It came on its own. Animals can sense love in the fingertips that caress them,' Mangasuri said.

'Are you saying I don't love it enough?' His voice was loud now.

'Don't you know?' Mangasuri asked back.

'Ah, you have all the love!' he screamed and threw his plate away. He swept the utensils off the table. Mangasuri and the daughter ran out of the room. The husband, now breathing furiously like a chimney, went to bed.

Scared by the commotion, the cat ran away. It never came back.

Grant Us Pardon, Saami

The ominous cries of the death birds reverberated across the village. It was the sixth death in a month. It had begun at the cattle shed of Maagaadu Sengaan and spread its wings to many households before finally reaching Manakaadu Ramasamy's field.

A trail of death, like the leap of a monstrous frog. The wails of Ramasamy's wife Poovayi pierced the darkness. Grief lay like a dog in front of every home and howled. Everyone worried, wondering if death's next leap would bring it to their house.

It had happened after sunset, so they decided to visit him that very night, carrying lanterns. Poovayi's unkempt hair, teary eyes and wailing sounds would move anyone. Beating her chest, she rolled on the floor and sobbed.

Hardly a month had passed since the calf had been born. It was a male calf and so was allowed to drink milk to its fill. It was a calf that could have been trained for any job. It had a good whorl of hair, the mark of its breed. It hadn't yet had its first bite of grass.

But it had started eating mud, instead, after the itching caused by drinking milk. They had covered its mouth with a basket to stop it from eating mud and allowed it to stray across the fields. When dawn broke, it was upbeat, running everywhere. The runs and leaps strengthened its legs.

'Is it a calf or a horse? It kicks up so much dust,' people had asked. Ramasamy had responded: 'Would I bring up my calf carelessly?'

Then it had begun to cry for its mother.

The cow that had birthed the calf would yield three or four measures of milk twice a day besides feeding the calf. It never tired of work either. It could walk tirelessly, even if tied to a plough or a vehicle. It was also expensive. It was as valuable as a sovereign of gold.

Why wouldn't Poovayi be sad at the loss of such a cow?

She wept as if she had lost her husband. No visitor could utter a word to her. Tears flowed even before they opened their mouths.

The house bore signs of its bereavement all over. There were cots outside, and the men were seated on rocks scattered beyond the house. The lanterns, their lights lowered, were like fireflies. Nobody had any idea of what to do next.

Some said the village was cursed. Some said it might be the handiwork of the soothsayer who had come to the village a month ago. He had arrived straight from the graveyard at midnight, made predictions for the village's families and prescribed them some rituals. But for want of money, the families had paid no heed. It could be his doing. Had he come in the month of Thai, he would have needed a cart to carry away his offerings. But now, after the humiliation of being sent away empty-handed, what had he left here?

Even the healer, who had a handy solution for every bovine affliction, couldn't identify the illness. He read every manuscript related to animal diseases through the night, with the help of a dim clay lamp. He made enquiries with every source he could find. He stayed overnight at the homes of those who had other manuscripts: it was believed that the solutions in these manuscripts would work only when they were opened and read in the light of a mud lamp. Sticking to this norm, the healer read each and every word.

There was no mention of this kind of disease anywhere. Could it be a new one? Wouldn't those who had lived before them for thousands of years know of it? They had discovered and written about everything. The healer had always maintained that it would suffice to interpret their notes. If he were helpless, who could the people turn to? What else could it be but the wrath of God?

It was unprecedented. When they were milking the cow at Sengaan's house, its hind legs began to tremble. Sengaan thought the cow was up to some gimmick and hissed at it. How does a cow that has begotten calves hesitate to yield milk? But as its legs kept trembling, its mouth started to froth. Barely five minutes had passed when the cow lowed in pain and fell. Its eyes were lifeless. The animal was instantly dead. The body shook from its weight and the impact of the fall.

It would have been some consolation if the cow had been unwell for a couple of days, had been tended to and then died. The sight of it falling over and dying in an instant was unbearable.

When the Dalit colony was informed, their people came in a crowd and carried the carcass away in their cart. The cow had to be trussed with a rope before it was shifted to the cart, which grew very heavy. They might have chopped the cow on the field and left with the pieces, but Ramasamy said the animal ought not to be chopped on the same field that it had once grazed.

It was evident that the cow had not died from

poisoning: they checked its tongue and said there was no sign of any toxins, even though instant deaths normally came about only because of poison. Had that been the case, the cow's tongue would have turned blue and its intestines would have popped out.

A cow would die, almost certainly, if it grazed on a stack of maize till its stomach was full. But where was one to find a stack of maize during summer on the hot fields? This cow would move away from the shed only when it wasn't tethered, that too when its rope was pulled at. It would stand still if its tether was tied even to a little plant. To which village was such an animal going to wander off to graze?

There had been no sign of the cow being sick. Its liver was healthy.

The next day, when the carcass-bearers came and said they couldn't find anything wrong with the cow, Sengaan's sorrow only deepened. Then, before he could be consoled by the possibility of the cow being hit by a bad spirit, another incident happened. The cow of Chinnaan from Vadakkadu; it was a similar incident. Death leapt from one field to another: Semmankaadu, Ottukaadu, Sarakkaadu – and now it was at Manakaadu's.

It became a phenomenon. A seemingly healthy cow's hind legs would tremble, it would begin to froth at its mouth, fall with a thud and die. How could anyone farm with cattle if two cows died every week? When it was discovered that only dairy cattle suffered the fate, people started to sell them. Since the news spread far and wide, buyers sought very low prices. Everyone was seized with the fear that the cattle might spread a new disease into other villages.

Money from the villagers' common fund was spent to hold rituals and appease the village deity. But the deaths didn't stop.

There was no solution left to try. The village decided to forget their differences and hold the annual festival: they would have nothing to do otherwise, except sit in front of houses that had lost a cow and offer condolences. If only they could know about a cow being infected beforehand they could do something to avert its fate. But there were no symptoms. How would they treat a disease that killed cows instantly?

The village head snapped at Ramasamy's wife Poovayi for wailing incessantly. 'Why is she wailing now? This is the sixth death. Your family isn't the only one to be affected. The entire village fears this disease. Ask her to stop crying, she might end up hurting herself. What are the women standing there doing? Console her. Is it enough to just watch her wail?' he shouted.

'Men will talk to each other and get over it. Women can get over things only by crying.'

The response irked the village head. 'What do you achieve by talking back to me?' he shouted again. The murmurs, however, continued.

Just then Vettukaattan emerged from the night and, looking at the porch filled with people, said: 'Every house is bereaved here, but that place is full of festivities.'

'What are you saying?' the village head asked Vettukaattan.

He told them about the goings-on in the Dalit colony. That neighbourhood wore the look of festivity on days they cooked meat. Those who did farm work would excuse themselves early to join the festivities. The celebrations were bigger if the cooking took place at night. The work of cutting the beef and partitioning it was to be done under the light of lanterns. The women would be waiting with ground masalas. A drinking session would start soon after the meat was mixed with masala and set to cook. There would be fights and commotion that settled in a moment.

'They are like a murder of crows. They stick together and always make noise. But we are scattered. Even if a person has to be heard by another, he has to shout at the top of his voice,' the village head would often say.

The sixth cow in three weeks. Every cow that died was

sturdy. The milch cows were particularly well taken care of. There were generous amounts of meat available for every family in the Dalit colony. The households would be counted when the beef was apportioned. Depending on the number of persons, some houses got more. The skin belonged to the colony as a whole.

Vettukaattan, who had gone by for some work, saw these celebrations and recounted them to the village. 'Every house got a large vessel full of meat,' he said. 'How could they finish it off in a day? Visit them tomorrow and you'll see the meat hanging outside each house. They'll preserve the meat in salt and cook it in gravy every day. They'll have meat even as a side dish. Even the children will be served meat.'

'Man, we're suffering stomach aches, but for them it's a huge stroke of luck. The gods have made it thus.' Ramasamy's voice was choked with sadness.

'Only moments before the cow died, Kandan fed it and told me to take good care of the milch cow. How could he chop and eat it now?' Poovayi cried again.

'Bears thinking about. Kandan should come, feed the cow, inform us about its condition and leave. Why should he advise us about it? Is he doing our farm work? Is he a labourer? Why is it his concern?' Muthaan asked. Everyone seemed to agree with him.

'He might have harmed the cow, tempted by its meat,' someone said.

Sengaan remembered that Raman from the colony had come to the cowshed on the day his cow had died. Maarappan suspected the presence of Kuppan from the colony on the day of his cow's death. All the six cowsheds had had visitors from the colony.

Some of these visitors were farm labourers, as it happened. 'They always came by the cowshed,' Vellappan said. And nobody had cared one way or another. But now it seemed that the cows had died soon after people of that colony had visited their cowshed. They had probably fed the cows with poisonous food. Or they had performed some black magic. Some of those people knew how to. There were soothsayers among them, too. They could have done something to the animals.

Usually, when the people of the colony took care of a dead cow, a man from the colony would visit the village to inform them of the cause of the cow's death, before they portioned it off for meat. But for the recent deaths, they would come only the day after and claim they knew no reason for the death. In the normal course of things, those people got dead cows only once or twice a year. Once or twice a month, they would go to the market, purchase a very lean calf and cook it. Each house would have to scrape the vessel to get enough meat and end up getting only the meat juices. They used to add water to the meat to stretch the juice.

It was now believed that the starving colony had decided to do something to the cows to feed themselves with meat.

A month earlier, Raman's son Rasu had jumped into the well in Sengaan's field for a swim. Sengaan had caught hold of him, tied his hands and feet and whipped him, letting him go only so as not to kill him. The moment he was set free, Rasu ran away like a calf, shouting: 'Dei Sengaan, you'll beat me, will you? Wait till I get back!'

Rasu had run away from the village after that and hadn't come back yet. His parents had come and supplicated in front of Sengaan.

'I'll behead him if I see him around here,' Sengaan lashed out.

There were rumours that Rasu had come back home in the thick of night. Maybe he had gotten up to some mischief to settle scores. How, otherwise, could a new disease have materialized all of a sudden? Who could invent a disease that had never been written about? Could anyone kill a milch cow just for its meat? Could it be the work of anyone with the slightest of mercy in their hearts?

It was decided that the people of the Dalit colony were to be summoned for an enquiry immediately. But was this some sort of business deal that required invitations through appropriate persons? The truth would come out only if these people were beaten on the same mouths that had savoured the cow meat before they were brought in for the enquiry.

What did the thief bring every night to kill the cows? Where was he now? They demanded answers for all these questions.

The night was still young, and the youth had gathered at the common grounds of the village. Everyone held sturdy sticks. Some carried the axles of a cart, some had the scaffolding taken off the racks of fodder and some brought the neem switches they kept at home to ward off insects. Every stick was tall enough to touch their throats. Their torches spread light across the grounds.

It was decided that only the youth would go. They were not to tarry, nor was any life to be lost. When they came back, they were to be driving at least one person in front of every stick.

The grounds fell silent, waiting to hear the noise that emerged from the colony after the youth left with the sticks. The village head and others seated on the stone bench did not talk to each other. The women and children sat in groups on the ground. When murmurs started, the village head cleared his throat and the murmurs stopped.

The dogs barked on the roads taken by the sticks. The colony was made up of forty or fifty small houses. The sticks laid siege as planned. At the sound of a whistle, the sticks rained blows on the colony. They broke everything, beginning with the pots on the stoves. The legs and the backs of the women in front of the stoves were beaten. The sticks dragged them to the ground by their hair and proceeded to violate their bodies. The children cried after one or two lashes and curled up in the corners of the huts.

The men heard the cries and screams of the children and women and rose from their drunk stupor, uncertain of what was happening. Some realized that the sticks were hovering over the colony as shadows and took refuge in the dark fields and shrubbery. The younger men couldn't immediately find weapons to counter the speed of the sticks and tried to fend them off with their hands. The older ones begged the sticks: 'Don't kill us, Saami. What did we do? Whatever it is, grant us pardon!'

They begged at the feet of the sticks, only to be kicked away and left to holler.

The mouths of the sticks had only two questions. 'What did you do?' and 'Where is he?' No one could respond to the ambiguous questions. Nor did the sticks wait for a response. They continued to work without a moment's rest. They landed blows on everything in front of them. The legs of the tethered goats and calves were injured, and they cried in pain. The dogs that had eaten the beef bones ran from the colony in fear. The cats hid themselves on the roofs, like rats. The pots were broken. The dried leaves on the rooftops fell when the sticks landed blows on the roof. The chickens flew atop the baskets and small trees and let out cries for help. Still the sticks raged. They landed bruises on the men they could get hold of. The colony was filled with the scent of blood.

When the sticks finally rested, the sound of weak laments rose everywhere. In front of each stick there was now a figure with hands bound. Some sticks were clever enough to have two figures in front of them. The figures couldn't say anything except 'Aiyo, Saami!'

'Walk!' the sticks ordered and pushed them.

The women who had run, walked and crawled to the ends of the colony stopped at the hooting of the sticks. Hands tied, the images walked with their bodies shrunk in pain. Some wore loincloths. Some were fully naked. The eyes hidden in the fields and shrubs were terrified to see the sticks pushing them. Nobody knew the reason.

Produced at the common grounds of the villagers, the

figures squealed and wept. The bodies that writhed in pain could express their agonies only in tears. The naked figures tried hard to hide themselves among the crowd. The sticks continued to threaten them. Sometimes, the long sticks hurt their ribs.

The village head seated at the centre of the ground began his enquiry. 'What did you do?' Just one question.

'We did nothing, Saami,' a figure said, still weeping.

A stick hit its back and shrieked: 'You didn't do anything?'

'Where is he?'

There was no answer to this question either. The figures could not even ask of whom the question was meant. 'We don't know, Saami,' a figure said, only to be hit on its leg by a stick. It collapsed with a sharp cry. Some figures realized the right thing to do was to be silent. They kept their heads down and did not open their mouths.

'What did you do?' The same question was repeated incessantly.

'Will they respond if you ask this way? Break their hands and feet, and then ask them!' a woman's voice rose from outside the circle.

'Where is that motherfucker Rasu?' asked a man standing next to the village head.

Grant Us Pardon, Saami

The figures immediately realized what the enquiry was about. They cried together: 'We have not seen him, Saami.'

'What was the poison he gave the cows?' The question was now clear.

'Nothing, Saami,' the figures said and fell to the ground. Their hands were folded.

'We know nothing, Saami! Grant us pardon, Saami!' they started begging.

The Game

Murugesh's father was always talking. Often, his words were advice. Sometimes, they took the form of wise counsel. At other times, he would chide Murugesh. The father also complained about the boy to his mother. The complaints were frequently about how Murugesh 'slept through the day and stayed awake all night'.

Murugesh would wake up at the earliest at eleven in the morning and have breakfast around noon. He would sleep again at around three in the afternoon, wake up at five and have lunch. He would take his bath around seven in the evening. After that, he would become active and start working at his computer. The work would go on forever. His parents would eat dinner around eight-thirty in the evening, at which time he would not yet be hungry. 'Let me eat later,' he would respond to his mother if she called him to dinner.

'Look at him, he won't sit with us for one meal,' his father would lament.

Murugesh would make himself dosas and eat them after his parents had gone to sleep. Then he would switch on his laptop, watch a movie or play music. Then he would start doing the work that he enjoyed most, unmindful of the time. At around two or three in the morning, he would fall asleep. On most days, neither the laptop nor the lights would be turned off.

He was a student of computer science, and this was his final year in college. He lived in a hostel but was home owing to the Covid-induced isolation. His mother made his favourite dishes but was upset that he wouldn't eat while the food was hot and fresh. Though it might appear that she sided with him when his father complained, her tone of voice also betrayed a sense of loyalty to his father. To treat perpetrator and complainant alike, and act without hurting either, is a special talent that mothers are bestowed with.

Murugesh was himself at a loss. He loved being awake at night rather than during the day; his world would come alive during night time. Yet he was disappointed about not talking enough with his parents. But there was no common ground with them. They couldn't keep up with the speed at which he spoke, or the things he talked about.

The parents had mastered the art of turning any conversation into an advice session. Seeing how impatient the father was at being cooped up at home, the mother suggested: 'Why don't you play cards or dayam (game of dice)?' She added another piece of advice to her list, this one to the father: 'Play with our son.'

The father used to play cards when he was young, but he wasn't sure he could now. All this while, he had pretended that he couldn't play. Knowing how to play cards would be a blow to his prestige. Clearly, there could be no dent in his moral compass.

Murugesh also knew how to play cards. While new kinds of games had cropped up online, cards remained significant at young men's clubs. But he didn't want to bring any of that home. His parents might be silent now, but at an opportune moment they would make a dig about him 'playing cards and neglecting studies'.

He also had some arrears to clear, so he concealed any inclination to play card games.

The decision went in favour of dice.

'Let's play Aeroplane Board; it'll be interesting. Also, we'll be able to play for a long time,' his father said.

Murugesh knew how to play dice; his grandmother had taught him. But he didn't know anything about this aeroplane board. His father had worked as a lorry driver for a short while and made halts at various places. He had made acquaintance with other lorry drivers and played different kinds of dice games during these halts. He would occasionally slip in a new game or two. Murugesh acquiesced when his father did this because it meant he could learn to play something new with the same dice.

The floor of their house was not made of lime mortar, which would make it easy to draw the board: it was slippery tiles all the way. Murugesh's father looked through his things, then picked out his wooden writing pad and drew a board behind it.

It was structurally different from the traditional dice game board. The father drew a human body, a round face and two hands that flew from the neck. The elbows were folded and raised. He drew six boxes on the right hand and six on the left. Another twelve boxes from the shoulders to the legs. Twelve more were attached to the feet. The boxes that began mid-waist and broke off on either side were square-shaped.

After rolling the dice, the counter was moved upwards from the feet. When it reached the waist, where the boxes

The Game

separated, it moved to the boxes on either side of the squares. There were a total of twelve such rounds.

The counter that moved away from one side of the waist would eventually reach the other side. From there, it would move to the neck and then to the hands, which were the last point. The first six moves were privileged. When the counter was there, it could not be overtaken. In these spaces, the counter was called the 'private dog'.

Similarly, if the counter entered the hand, it entered another privileged space. The object could not be overtaken here. It was called a 'fruit dog' in this zone. The rest of the spaces were common, and the counter was called the 'green dog' in these zones. The green dogs on either side would run in opposite directions. One would defeat the other. If there was a hill, it would climb it. There were twelve dogs on either side.

The structure and the rules of the game excited Murugesh. *This will make for a good computer game*, he thought. But he wanted to learn it properly before making any attempt to create one. Enthused, he got into the game.

On day one, they sat down to it after lunch. The game continued even after Murugesh's mother called them to dinner. They played only two rounds. But since each side had twelve dogs, they defeated each other and restored the dogs to their original spaces over and over again. And the game went on.

His father frequently reminded Murugesh of the rules. When he faltered on numbers because the board was unfamiliar, his father pointed out his mistakes. His father himself had had practice with the game, of course, and knew strategies to defeat the opposite counters. He was able to safeguard his counters from being defeated by his son's, while defeating his son's counters. After each defeat, he laughed and celebrated. He called out to his wife to proclaim his victory: he knew mothers always sided with their sons.

'He's young and gullible. But he's going learn the game quickly and defeat you,' she would say.

Murugesh was not worried about victories and defeats. He was keener to learn the nuances of the game. In one version, the rule allowed a counter coin to jump over its opponent when it was not on the hill. But another, harder, version of the game disallowed it.

He thought about how to write a program for this game. His father won both games that first day.

The game continued the following day. They sat down after breakfast. The father was proud of the previous day's victories when he sat down to play. But halfway through the game he realized that Murugesh was not what he had

The Game

been yesterday. On his first day he had played defence, trying to secure his counters by moving them to the hill. But on this day, he started playing offence, placing his counter in between, obstructing his father's. The father's counters couldn't cross his borders and were defeated. Somehow, the father managed to win the game.

They played another game after lunch. Murugesh began the game on the offence. His counters never moved to the hill. He kept them in the open and confronted his father. At one point, six of the father's counters were defeated at the same time. The single digit on the dice that had the power to restore them wasn't turning up, either. The father lost despite using all his might.

It was Murugesh's first victory in the game. He examined it from different angles and then celebrated it.

Anticipating her son's victory, his mother had already made gulab jamuns from leftover flour bought long ago. She served the sweets to both father and son. The son relished it. The father chided his wife. 'What will we do if we catch a cold in this Covid season? They say the cold will affect the lungs. And this flour is old. Don't you have any sense of responsibility?'

'Don't worry about losing to our son,' the wife said, handing over his plate. 'You can win tomorrow. Have this, don't fuss.'

He didn't budge. 'I've won three games in two days. He's won just one – and look at you, celebrating! I don't want this. I'm already worried about my health; I cannot have this and worry more.'

'Fine, I'll keep it in the fridge. Son, eat it tomorrow,' she said.

'Keep it, Amma. I'll have it after I've won tomorrow's game as well,' Murugesh said.

Their dinner conversations were about the game. The father couldn't handle their excitement. *Where did I go wrong?* he wondered.

That night, Murugesh began to write code for the game and went to sleep around dawn. He was still sleeping when his parents had their breakfast – at around ten in the morning.

'Wait, let me wake him up. Won't you start your game after breakfast?' the mother said. To Murugesh, it felt like he was hearing those words in a dream. He was still sleepy, but excited to start the game.

'He was awake a long time and is in deep sleep now. Why do you want to wake him up now? It's just a game, we can play it tomorrow as well,' he could hear his father responding to his mother.

The Obstinate One

Murugesh stopped talking, even at the workplace. He had many friends in his old work group. He left the group simply because he didn't want to face any of them, and joined a new work group. He resolved not to befriend anyone in this new group. He was adamant about the change, though his old friends repeatedly pleaded with and apologized to him. He would step out of his home just in time to get to work. He would not wait for even a moment after the day was over to start his vehicle. He would come straight home and refresh himself.

He also changed houses. An astrologer to whom his father-in-law took him had said that north-facing houses were more suitable for him. He found just such a house and moved in, even though it meant paying more rent.

He took up a job that was within twenty kilometres of his house so that he could reach home within half an hour. He would also work only until five in the evening. He wouldn't stay longer even if the day's work could be completed in just another thirty minutes. He would ask others to finish the job, and leave without waiting for their response. Once at home, he would step outside only the next morning.

He had never been this kind of person – a homebody. His world used to be out of doors, and home simply a place he could come to sleep for a while. But a certain incident had changed things.

Murugesh laid sheet roofs for a living. He had started with asbestos sheets and learnt the ropes of the work from there. The sheets were the choice for people who couldn't afford to lay flooring for their house or use tiles for roofs. They were the kind of sheets that absorbed the heat and trapped it inside houses. Laying sheet roofs was a difficult job. The sheets were very heavy even if three people lifted them together. One had to be careful when one climbed the roof to place the sheets. Even a small, invisible crack, if inadvertently stepped on, would break the sheets. The person who stepped on the sheet would fall through. Murugesh himself had been witness to such an accident, when a fifty-five-year-old man had broken his leg and never been able to return to work.

Shocked by that accident, Murugesh had temporarily

quit his job and had started working at a poultry farm. The town had many poultry farms, and he chose one run by someone who treated him well. His job was to clean the chickens' waste, feed them and collect the eggs. He was averse to the smell of the waste and medicines.

But even as he was thinking of shifting jobs again, the making of sheet roofs underwent a drastic change. Tin sheets, also known as colour sheets and Japan sheets, entered the market, and many people began to prefer these to asbestos. Their arrival did away with the practice of laying sheets using coconut and palm fronds. It was nothing like laying asbestos, he was told; laying tin sheets was way easier. Tin sheets became omnipresent. They were used for cattle sheds, goat houses, large godowns, houses and terraces.

A group of five or six boys got together to go into the business of laying tin sheets. They invited Murugesh to join their group.

One day, Murugesh tried his hand at this job and took a liking to it. He was used to climbing roofs anyway. The tin sheets didn't break even if they were stepped on by mistake: they might only give in slightly. He was relieved that there wasn't any chance of an accident. He didn't have to carry heavy loads either: the tin sheets were so light that they could fly. They still required two persons to pick up the sheet on either end. You still had to be careful when handling the corners of the sheets: they were sharp.

Murugesh took a liking to the colours of the sheets. He liked that they did not transmit heat inside the houses, though they would make noise in the rains.

He liked the job and continued to do it. The pay made him content too.

He was introduced to many friends in the process of laying tin sheets. It was such a happy time that he felt like he was back in college again. He had only been able to fit into an English literature course after the twelfth standard because he had scored low marks in his exams. He was told that he could shift courses after joining, but it had never happened. In his first semester, he could only clear the Tamil paper. He was not sad, though, because most of the students met with the same fate. He decided to enjoy his college days. At the end of his time in college, the papers he had cleared were in single digits, and those in which he had arrears were in doubles. The college celebrated the fact that at least one student from the entire lot had passed and got a degree.

Murugesh never went back to college after that, but the three years he had spent there had filled him with happiness. This job gave him a similar vibe.

His friends watched new movies. They went to various

restaurants in town. Occasionally, they also went to the waterfalls nearby and bathed there. On salary day, they would get beers. They bought new mobile phones too. They went to cultural festivals in the months of Maasi and Panguni. They would talk about women with excitement. They were joyous days.

Ever since he had started the tin roofing job, his parents had stopped taking his salary. Both his elder brothers were married, and it was his turn next, so his parents told him to save up for his wedding. He could get married as soon as he managed to save up some money. If his parents decided to look out for a girl, it would only take a month. He was interested in getting married. So he cut down on his expenses and started saving up. In six months, he saved fifty thousand rupees. His parents, who always asked about his savings, didn't this time. Boldly, he told them how much he had saved. His father would contribute something, having made plans to take an advance from his employer.

One day, his father told him about four or five girls who were prospective brides and asked him to choose one. The father had already collected details about these girls, checked that their horoscopes matched Murugesh's and so on. He told Murugesh the background of each family too.

Murugesh observed each girl, from a distance, in

different settings and took a liking to the girl in the tailor shop. She was a little dark, just like the colour of tender mango leaves before they turned green, as if she would become bright when you wiped her off. She smiled brightly against a backdrop of salwar suits, stitched and lined up. The smile left him impressed. He thought she could make some money from home, since she knew tailoring. She appeared smart too.

The family had three daughters and a son. Two daughters were already married. The girl's father worked on the same poultry farm where Murugesh had temporarily worked. He knew him well: not a fussy man. He was a hard worker too.

The families decided to get them married in January, in the month of Thai, and then talked about where they would live. Of the family's two houses in town, his eldest brother occupied one. The other brother lived in a different town. The house in which Murugesh and his parents lived had only one room and a kitchen. The parents would have to leave if the newlyweds lived there. There was nothing available to rent in town.

The girl's father came up with an idea. The poultry farm had no caretaker at night. They had to arrange for someone on a daily basis or have someone from the owner's house come to stay the night. The owner and his family had once lived on the property, looking after their farmland. After their income grew, they had decided to move to the city for the children's higher education. Their family bought three plots in a suburb and built a huge bungalow. They had three cars.

Their large, tile-roofed house in the fields was still vacant. The family stayed there occasionally and used it as a storehouse. At the back of the house was a long, curving room meant for their workers who could live there with their families while taking care of the farmlands and the poultry. But that too was empty.

The family would give it for free. They wouldn't need to look for night duty if a family lived there, after all. There was no water shortage. Murugesh and his wife could even use the vegetables that grew on the land. They could forage fallen coconuts. There would be no dearth of eggs. Murugesh could do farm or poultry work on days he didn't have a roofing job: the farm was constantly in need of workers. Even if he went away on a job, the father-in-law would come to work every day and could meet his daughter. Murugesh could live problem-free.

He knew that this owner would treat him with respect. The field was also close to the town, which was good: he aspired to provide his children with a good life. He had lots of dreams for his children. Given the facility and the costs, the arrangement sounded good.

The poultry owner agreed immediately. He had been looking for night guards. A young man like Murugesh would be very helpful. 'Even if you travel, make sure you return by nightfall,' the owner said. 'If you cannot, make alternative arrangements.'

The couple moved in three days after their wedding. The long room was full of shelves, and felt big even after they had stored all their things. But it had no dividing walls. That made it difficult for anybody to stay over. Murugesh's father-in-law came up with an idea and made a divider from coconut fronds. The space beyond the divider was now a bedroom.

Murugesh's wife liked the house. For the first couple of days, relatives came visiting. But after that, they were left alone. They were able to enjoy the privacy meant for newly wed couples. They talked to each other freely, laughed aloud and fooled around. They cooked together and fed each other.

They kissed and hugged one another when he left for work. Some days, the hugs were so tight that he had to stay back at home, skipping work. He had a habit of twirling his thick moustache upwards. That became her plaything.

She would twist it downwards. Then, 'Doesn't look good,' she would say and twist it upwards again.

He loved playing with the hair by her ears with his lips. Whenever he stepped out, it was as if he was leaving half of his body behind, so much was she a part of his body and mind.

The nights were glorious. One solitary night, he placed his hand on her stomach and asked: 'Has our baby arrived?'

'Are you in a hurry?' she asked, in return.

'Yes, I want to have ten babies.' He smiled.

She menstruated ten days after the wedding. 'What happened?' he asked, upset.

'You talk as if we've been married for years. Will you leave me if we don't have a baby?' she cried.

He spent the whole night comforting her, telling her she was more important than anything. She lay with her face in his hands. Her tears flowed through his palms. He had to spend the entire night wiping her tears and kissing her. After that, he never spoke of a child.

The following month, her period was late. When she told him, he wanted to go to the hospital and get her checked up. She refused, saying that periods could sometimes be up to two weeks late, and that they ought to wait. He agreed but was certain that the baby was coming. He touched her stomach gently.

Placing an ear to her stomach, he said: 'Doesn't it sound like two babies?'

'Yes, I will deliver ten babies all at once and die. You can keep them and pet them endlessly.'

He felt he shouldn't have been in a hurry and tried to act natural.

When he returned from work one evening, she had made aromatic kesari and gulab jamun. He loved sweets, and she made them well. She had the habit of surprising him, and he thought this was one of those days.

But she twitched his ear and said: 'You are a father now.' She had gone with her mother to the hospital for a checkup.

He showered her with love meant for a lifetime.

'Don't I know you? This is not for me, it is for your child,' she complained.

'*Our* child,' he corrected her.

The entire month turned out to be happy for them. He wondered why she didn't have morning sickness. 'Not everyone gets it,' she explained. 'Sometimes, it takes three months.'

He made sure that his weight didn't overwhelm her. On full moon days, they sat near the well and talked about their child for hours. He bought beer with her permission, and caressed her in a drunken stupor. He forced her to drink, too, and wouldn't listen when she refused saying it smelled bad. But when she said it would affect the child, he immediately stopped.

It was April, the month of Chithirai. Temple festivals were under way in neighbouring towns. His friends in the roofing business were talking and laughing among themselves. When it appeared that they were elbowing him out, he asked what they were discussing secretly, and tried to join in.

'You wouldn't fit in,' a friend said. Another added: 'You get to see it up close every day, why bother about this?'

When he probed further, he found out that they were talking about a dance performance they had seen at one of the temple festivals. The organizers had likely obtained permission by giving written assurance that the dances wouldn't be obscene. Yet, they had sometimes bordered on obscenity, and the last performance had been the culminating point.

This is what they were discussing, and when they found out he was interested in joining them, they told him that he couldn't come. 'As a married man, you wouldn't fit in,' they said, and laughed again.

He had to show that nothing had changed, that he remained the same. 'Let me know if there's a performance today,' he said stubbornly. 'I will join in.' He prayed and hoped there was no performance on that day.

But they said there was one that day and named the town. They laughed again when he began thinking.

'You won't come, I know,' someone said.

'That upturned moustache has drooped after marriage,' said another.

'Have you come anywhere with us these three months? Don't bluff again,' someone said provocatively.

It was salary day. Their plan was to collect wages, get a couple of beers, eat some food and go to the town in question.

'I will come today,' Murugesh told them firmly. He stepped away and called her from his cell phone, telling her that a friend had invited him to a family function, and it wouldn't look good if he didn't accept. He said he would finish dinner and be back by ten and suggested that she go to his parents in town; he would bring her back on his return.

'Will you come back by ten?' she asked over and over. He was unusually irritated.

'Can't you listen?' he shouted at her. 'It might take more time than that even. That's why I am asking you to stay with my parents.' He cut the call and realized he had never been rude to her before. He was upset but told himself that he would placate her that night.

He went with his friends. Normally he would have had

one beer. On that day, he had one and a half. 'You haven't changed, Murugesh.' A friend patted his back.

They ate at their usual eatery. The town was not close by, as he had imagined. They drove forever. When he worried about the distance, someone pointed out that the next day was a holiday. It was ten when they reached the town. She called him. 'It is ten already. How long will it take?'

He said that they had been able to get their salaries only by eight and had just arrived at their friend's place. He told her not to worry – he would come and wake her up.

Just then he realized that she hadn't gone to his parents' place and was still at the poultry farm. She said the owner had visited in the evening and stayed until nightfall. She didn't want the owner to think that there was no one around to guard the place and had dropped the idea of going to his parents'.

He didn't want to reveal his anger at her staying alone. 'Fine, bolt the door and sleep. I will come and wake you up, don't worry,' he said.

'I'm not worried,' she replied. 'Aren't I familiar with this place? Still, come soon.'

But he couldn't return soon. The performance started only at eleven. He was worried that the others would tease him more if he decided to leave midway after being so adamant about joining them. *Anyway, the place is familiar as she says. Let her sleep, I will go and wake her up*, he told himself.

The performance started with a spiritual song. A woman dressed as a goddess danced. 'They're fully covered in the first song. And remove their clothes fully in the last,' one friend said.

Perhaps everyone thought so. There was a TASMAC shop just by the festival venue. It was open beyond its regular hours since it was a festival day. The gang bought beer bottles at room temperature, one for each.

It was Murugesh's second beer of the day, though there had been a gap between drinks, and nothing much happened. When the performance picked up steam, he forgot everything. After the last dance was over, and he had dropped his friend en route, he reached home at two in the morning.

Just then, he felt a weird desire. *Didn't she say she was not afraid? Let me try and scare her,* he thought. He turned off his bike when entering the field. He pushed the vehicle slowly, against a strong wind, and parked it in front of the owner's house. Then he went around to his house and knocked on the door.

The Obstinate One

Before opening the door, she asked: 'Who is this?' He didn't respond. He knocked again.

'Who is this?' she asked again. This time the fear was evident in her voice.

He didn't respond. He folded a knuckle down and gently knocked again. 'Bad spirits! Don't play with me. I will tell him tomorrow and do away with you. Keep shut till I go to the bathroom and come back, okay?' she was speaking into the wind while opening the door.

'Blahhh!' he roared and jumped in front of her.

'Aiyo!' she screamed and dropped to the floor.

'It's me, just me, don't be afraid' he yelled. He hugged her and patted her on the back.

The next moment, she held her stomach and screamed: 'Amma...!'

Drops of blood scattered near his feet.

Dog

When Murugesh woke up and stepped out, the woman was sitting alone in a corner of the porch.

He summoned his sister to show her. 'Take care of her,' he said to the sister. The house had a toilet and a bathroom, only for the women's use. The men went to the fields to bathe and to relieve themselves as usual. Still, a newcomer would feel reluctant to make enquiries.

'I will; you can leave,' his sister replied carelessly.

He hadn't been able to catch a proper glimpse of them when the woman and Ramesh had arrived last evening. Her face shone like a black grape, with a bit of white. Ramesh had a body that looked like he was carrying a vanaspati tin from shoulders to waist. *He had managed to get an amazing woman*, Murugesh thought.

He hesitated to ask the woman about Ramesh's whereabouts. Ramesh had trusted him enough, as a friend, to bring a woman from two districts away to his house. How could he have turned the couple away? The previous night they had spoken for a long time and gone to bed late. Murugesh had also had to placate people at home, given the situation. That was why he had woken up late this morning.

Ramesh had likely gone to the fields. *We can ask him when he is back*, Murugesh thought and walked away.

Murugesh, who belonged to the hills, had lived in the district headquarters for a few years as a student. He had roomed with his friends in a two-room house with a tiled roof in the middle of a field. Initially, the landowner had occupied this house, but his family had built a bigger one and left. By renting it out to students, they were not only earning some money, but had also sorted out the security of the property.

To cover his expenses during this time, which included rent, food and transport, Murugesh had taken up various part-time jobs. One of these stints had entailed a few months working at a street food stall. He would work from six in the evening to eleven at night, serving food and making takeaway parcels. He didn't have to worry about dinner at this job: he could eat as much as he liked. If he carried leftover sambhar home, his lunch the following day would be sorted too – all he had to do was cook

Dog

himself some rice. The stall saw a large turnout between eight and nine in the night. His hands would begin to ache from serving and packing food. From nine onwards, the crowd would be manageable. It was a difficult job, but very helpful in its way.

That was where he met Ramesh. Ramesh had also come to the eatery to work: the owner was acquainted with Ramesh's father. His mother had not been keen on sending him to this job. But Ramesh had taken it up willingly because he could earn some money while getting to eat different kinds of dishes every night. Ramesh studied at a different college from Murugesh. He lived in a town nearby, and he could take a bus every day to go to class. The last bus would come around ten-thirty at night. Since there was a stop close to the shop, Ramesh could see the bus coming and run to catch it.

They had both been studying chemistry. That had brought them closer. Sometimes, Ramesh would stay over at Murugesh's place. That would be on days when Ramesh's mother travelled out of town to go to some function or the other. His mother wouldn't let him stay at someone else's house if she were around.

Everyone who stayed with Murugesh belonged from the hills. Ramesh once said, somewhat wistfully, that he had never been to the hills. When they had held a festival at the local temple, Murugesh had sought permission from his mother and taken Ramesh with him to his town. Ramesh had stayed for four days.

Everything about the hills had surprised him. 'I have never seen any of these,' he kept saying over and over. For the first time, he tried a bit of hill arrack. 'Isn't this wrong?' he asked innocently. 'My mother would burn me alive if she came to know of this.'

The four days of his stay had forged a stronger connection between them.

Murugesh had also visited Ramesh's home town. Ramesh was the only son of his parents, and the family indulged him. His mother spent all her free time taking care of him. When she was around, she wouldn't let him pick up a glass of water for himself. 'Wouldn't your hands ache, darling?' she would ask.

'What would your mother say if she sees your hands aching from packing food?' Murugesh would tease him.

Ramesh's mother demanded that he return home every night, no matter what. He had violated the edict in forging a friendship with Murugesh and visiting his hill town. But in a few days of staying at their home, Murugesh earned the confidence of Ramesh's mother.

In his last term, Murugesh had four papers to rewrite. He wasn't hopeful of clearing them. He filled his heart with memories of the city and returned home. Back there, he worked the family farm, sometimes cutting tubers.

Ramesh had two pending papers, both in English. He was confident of clearing them – if he could just stay home and study for six months.

The two of them spoke often over the phone. Murugesh had arrears in two main papers and two English papers. Ramesh promised to help him with the main subjects. He said if Murugesh would come home a week before the examinations, Ramesh could teach him all the important lessons.

But Murugesh was more interested in farming than in education. 'Let us see,' he had said, non-committal.

When studying for his English arrears, Ramesh had also done something else. He had fallen in love with a woman living in the house opposite his. They belonged to the same caste and were related, too. Yet, people living on opposite sides of the street were bound to be enemies. The families didn't get along well and were not on talking terms.

Love, of course, was blind. Everyone at her house would leave to go to work during the day. It was the same at his house. When left alone, their eyes had met. They had started talking in gestures and soon started talking directly.

Her parents had already found a groom for her. His mother wouldn't accept her, come what may, any more than her parents would accept Ramesh. They felt the families would come around after they got married. Together, they had come to Murugesh's home, in the only town Ramesh knew besides his own.

Ramesh had called Murugesh to tell him he was coming to his place, and that he needed help. 'I do not know anyone else,' he had said. He hadn't mentioned that he was bringing a woman along. Murugesh got to know of it only after they both arrived.

He had to help because Ramesh trusted him. They had talked and the couple stayed with him overnight. Everything else could be decided the following morning.

Murugesh's family asked the couple to inform their respective households. The woman handled it better. She called her father and told him the news – she and Ramesh would be back after the wedding, and that they needn't worry. She did not tell them of her whereabouts, and switched her phone off after the conversation.

Ramesh stepped away to speak to his mother and came back, upset. 'Mother is weeping,' he said. Murugesh consoled him and bade him sleep.

Murugesh himself slept poorly through the night. He gave Ramesh his bed, and slept on the floor. The woman slept with his mother and sister in their room. Several thoughts ran through his mind. He had never been involved in a love marriage of this sort before. He wondered if he should get them married at the local temple or if he should take them to the registrar's office. He thought of getting them married at a temple in the foothills. Maybe the families ought to be invited, persuaded and convinced to have the couple married in their own town.

He wallowed for long, and finally fell into a deep slumber near dawn.

Ramesh, who had already been here earlier, was familiar with the outer fields. He had probably decided against waking Murugesh. If Murugesh were nervous enough to lose his sleep, how could Ramesh have slept well? He had probably woken up early and left for the fields. Murugesh's friends, whom he might have met along the way, would also have remembered him.

Murugesh went to the fields to relieve himself, and washed his feet in a small stream that ran just through the middle of the lands. Then he looked around. Ramesh was nowhere in sight.

'Ramesh . . . Ramesh?' he called out. His voice echoed across the trees and soared in the air. There was no response. Could he have gone back to the house? By which path?

There were many paths through the fields that led to Murugesh's home.

Murugesh decided that Ramesh had returned home and left.

She was still seated on the porch. Her face appeared troubled: a woman who had left her home would, obviously, be more confused than the man. 'Where is Ramesh?' he asked his mother.

'Didn't he go with you?' his mother asked. His father knew nothing either. He asked the woman. 'I don't know,' she said, shocked.

Could he have lost his way in town?

Occasionally, one could sight a wild boar in the hills. It would run away if it saw a human being and attack only when it came into direct confrontation with one. There could be no other problem otherwise.

'Wait, let me check the fields again,' he said.

'Check if his bag is still here,' his father, always suspicious about people, said. Would someone who had eloped with a woman abandon her and run away?

But his father's suspicion won. Ramesh had left town.

Witnesses had seen him leave early in the morning, by the five o'clock bus. He had taken the same bus home during his previous visit. His phone was switched off. Murugesh paced up and down and finally came home and

Dog

sat down on the porch, dejected. He could hear the woman weeping inside. The villagers had gathered. The father was delivering updates about the turn of events.

'Coward. How could he leave a woman he had brought with him?'

'Didn't he like her when he brought her here? What changed now?'

Someone was mad enough to spit and it splashed on Murugesh's face.

'He is so disgusting, and he's your friend?' asked his friend Vinoth, lifting his head and looking into Murugesh's eyes.

'He's abandoned her. Should we get her married to Murugesh?' His friends laughed.

He didn't care about Ramesh having left home. But the woman who had trusted him was still here. What could they do with her?

A woman who went inside asked her all kinds of questions. 'How did you trust someone like him?'

'Whoever it is, a man shouldn't be so deeply trusted. What would you have done if he had abandoned you at a bus stop?'

'People like him would not hesitate to sell you off.'

'Were you wearing any jewellery? Is it still with you or have you given it to him?

'Would anyone abandon their parents like this?'

The women gathered to chide and question her. She didn't respond to any of them, simply weeping. Murugesh's mother took her inside and asked his sister to keep her company. Ramesh might have found himself in some kind of emergency, perhaps, but shouldn't he have informed them that he was leaving her with them for a couple of days? He could even have sent Murugesh or someone else to talk to his parents. Could any person simply up and leave without letting a soul know?

Murugesh was worried, not knowing who to respond to and what to say. People asked him, in direct and indirect ways, about Ramesh and the woman's caste. 'Would they fall in love only after learning of each other's caste?' he asked, irritated. He knew their caste, but he didn't want to reveal it at this point.

'Did you call him?' Vinoth asked and Murugesh told him.

'He has brought a woman and abandoned her here. How long will you sit like this?' Vinoth said. 'Let's try to drop her back to her place.'

Ramesh's phone was constantly switched off. Inside the house, the woman was lying down, her body curled up, but she got up instantly when Murugesh asked her for her phone. She looked for it and switched it on. They called her home. Her brother took the call. There was a clamour on the other side.

From this conversation, they were able to glean some information about what had happened.

On the phone the night before, Ramesh's mother had threatened to kill herself if he didn't come home the next morning: 'You will only see my corpse if you don't leave her there and come home.' The threat had worked, and he had left her to return home the morning after. He had left without telling Murugesh because he knew the latter wouldn't have let him go. Both families had been fighting when Ramesh had got home. Ramesh's mother claimed that her son was innocent and the woman had bewitched him. In response, the woman's mother had called Ramesh a wastrel who sat at home and had despoiled her daughter.

The fight took a turn for the worse.

The woman's family proceeded to physically assault Ramesh, asking where he had abandoned their daughter. The entire town turned against him. Who would speak up for someone who had taken a woman away only to desert her somewhere? Afraid, he told them the truth and was spared only after they were convinced that she was in a safe place. Then, the families entered a discussion and decided to get the two married: they were, after all, related.

In the chaos, Ramesh simply hadn't been able to call Murugesh and let him know of the developments.

The woman's brother said to Murugesh: 'Brother, it will take time for us to come there and bring my sister back. Could you please bring her home to us? We've fixed the wedding date for tomorrow, and we haven't finished preparing for it. Everything is sorted, brother.'

Ramesh spoke to Murugesh: 'I am sorry, da. My mother said she would hang herself, and I know you wouldn't have let me go if I had told you. I dreamt of my mother lying as a corpse throughout the night, da. I couldn't sleep. I was certain she would be safe in your house. Please don't take this amiss. I really wanted to call and let you know. I thought of convincing my mother, then bringing her here and getting married. But the minute I turned up, they were fighting. I couldn't talk to you before this.'

Murugesh thought he should meet Ramesh in person, slap him hard and rebuke him for making a fool of Murugesh in his home town. He cursed him in his heart as he boarded the bus with her. She sat with the women on the bus without uttering a word. They exchanged a word or two only when they changed buses. Murugesh's mother had forced her to eat before they left. She ate nothing on the way and asked only for a bottle of water. Murugesh didn't insist that she eat, either.

Dog

It was well after noon when they reached Ramesh's town, where things had calmed down after the storm. The wedding was to be held the following day. They were worried that Ramesh's mother would scuttle the marriage if it were held any later.

As soon as Murugesh and the woman turned into his street, Ramesh came running and held Murugesh's hands. 'Forgive me, da, please forgive me,' he kept pleading. Murugesh couldn't recollect any of the words he had chosen to rebuke him. He should have slapped him hard before he started talking, but everything changed after he started talking.

'Fine, it's fine,' Murugesh said, and started to console Ramesh.

They came to her house. Ramesh let go of Murugesh's hand and reached for hers.

'Ramya!' he called and held her hands.

'Let me go, you dog!' she said and freed her hand from his.

Standing on the steps of her home, she looked out at everyone and said: 'Don't ask me to marry this dog. I didn't elope with this dog. I went to my brother's place. Nothing more.'

Hunger

Murugesh asked his wife to attend a family wedding with him. He had to travel for three hours from his village to get to the venue, and it would take his wife about an hour from her workplace. The wedding turned out to be an occasion for the couple to meet.

He farmed on a meagre one and a half acres of land. He had a couple of cows and some goats. Murugesh didn't waste a drop of water from the well. He put a price on every single thing he harvested. All this helped him make ends meet. His wife was a graduate and had trained as a typist in college. She had given a government examination prior to her wedding but married Murugesh before the results were out. By the time they were posted, she was busy with married life.

She got a typist's job. They made every attempt to get her posted near their village. He met many people to this end but was told that her department and location would be decided based on consultation and that she ought to accept wherever she was posted. They were told, furthermore, that she could get a transfer to somewhere near their village after a short while.

She was posted to a town four hours away from theirs. They had no option. She had to take it up. They would catch hold of a politician later and secure a transfer.

She invited him to join her in the village to which she was posted. What more could he possibly earn from farming? In any case, his mother could take care of the land, she said. They could rent a house together, and he could get a local job. He could even choose not to work.

He was sad at the prospect of living away from his wife just a few days after they had been married and considered her proposal. But he couldn't abandon farming, or his cattle and goats. Even if he decided to go with her, it would be difficult to start from scratch all over again. Amma couldn't handle the farm without him.

It was also a matter of pride when it came to living off his wife's salary. He could well have three meals a day and while away his time sleeping. But would he sleep well without doing any work? Though he could cook, how much could he cook for two people? What else could he do in the city? He had grown up wandering through fields and woods. He couldn't shrink himself in a city and work there.

He offered words of solace to his wife and got her admitted to a hostel in the town.

She worked in the Revenue Department, which had no official working hours. Weekends weren't guaranteed either. The government might announce a welfare scheme after which ministers, even the chief minister, came to visit the villages. During those times, the Revenue Department worked night and day. The employees had to come in to work even on holidays. So, she could come home to Murugesh's village only when she was free. Sometimes, she would visit two weeks in a row. Sometimes, it would take a month or two. This left her frustrated about her choice of department. A regular office job should ideally be nine to five. In what kind of job does one have to stay back until eight or nine? But her colleagues in the department were used to this and she had no other option.

After her visits, he would be upset for the next few days, thinking of her. Sometimes, he even considered moving in with her. *What kind of a life is this?* He sighed to himself. It still felt like he didn't know her well enough.

'It has been a year since the wedding,' his mother would rue. 'Nothing has borne fruit yet. How would it? They don't even live together.'

He would try to distract himself with work, but the goat, the cattle, the trees and even the earth reminded him of her face. What was he to do?

She almost always avoided going home on holidays. She felt bad for him, of course, but the stress from work and travel ended up tiring her out, and he didn't understand. Her body was his plaything. She couldn't sleep a wink too long in the mornings. Her mother-in-law's murmured taunts were a violent wake-up call. When she was home, she had to do all the chores. It didn't matter to the mother-in-law that she also toiled at her workplace. And the chores didn't stop with cooking: she would have to clean the house, wash the sheets and more. It was as if the mother-in-law let the chores accumulate so she could come and do them.

Things were better if a Friday or a Monday turned out to be a government holiday. She would sometimes take an additional day off. She would finish all the chores in the first two days and get some rest on the third day. It made her return more comfortable. In the town where she worked, she had nothing to do except go to office. She could sleep a bit longer in the mornings. She could go to the office at eleven in the morning too. If there was no chance for an additional day off, she would stay back at the hostel.

Hunger

'Can't you come this week?' He would sound miserable every week. With a heavy heart, she would tell him it was not possible because she had work.

So Murugesh didn't let go of any chance to meet. Sometimes, he created opportunities to do so. This relative's wedding was one such. He asked the relatives if accommodation was made available for the guests. He told them that his wife was coming, and that they would need a separate room. He had requested her to join him.

'I want to see you, at least your face,' he told her. Not a day passed without him cursing her job. There was no vacancy in their district. They had to approach a politician. But when would it happen?

She reached the wedding hall before he arrived: she had taken special permission from her workplace and left early. There were many familiar faces among the wedding guests. When they asked her about Murugesh, they also asked about how they were living apart. Untiringly, she told everyone that he was on the way. He had thought that she would come only after work, and had taken a bus accordingly. They had discussed everything, but not the time of her arrival. Neither had she expected her office to give her permission. There hadn't been much work on that particular day, so her superior had let her go when she had sought permission.

Murugesh's bus stopped at every little bus stop. A whole crowd was going to the wedding. At every stop, he looked up wondering if it was his. None of his calculations about reaching the next stop early worked. The journey took its own sweet time. His heart travelled faster, and was looking at her already. He called her every five minutes and updated her on his location.

'Fine,' she answered each time.

'Don't eat, okay?' he told her. 'We will eat together.'

How would it be possible to eat together at a wedding? she wondered.

Only the bride and the groom had rooms at the wedding hall. The rituals would be conducted through the night, and close relatives would only sleep a little, in the hall itself. The bed sheets and mats were lined up in a corner. The plastic chairs could be removed and mats for sleeping could be spread on the floor as needed. The hall had ten bathrooms and toilets.

The relatives sat in circles and started repeating old tales. She didn't know which circle to join, and stayed aloof.

Accommodation for certain important guests had been arranged at a hotel nearby. It had two big common rooms, each of which could accommodate at least ten people. She left her bag in the common room meant for women, got

Hunger

dressed and went to the hall. Her eyes were at the entrance looking for him even as she engaged with anyone who asked her questions.

She was very hungry and thinking of eating her meal alone when he appeared. With his own bag he had brought along another, one filled with goodies for her. He was all smiles.

'Where is our room?' he asked her. She told him the details of the sleeping arrangements.

'But I had asked them for a separate room. Shouldn't you have found out more?' he said and started looking for someone without waiting for her response. She was still hungry. She rested the bag he had brought at her feet. Someone came and asked if he was yet to come. Many others asked if she had had her meal.

He couldn't find the person he was looking for in the hall and came back to her. 'Where did he go?' he asked her. She wasn't familiar with the person he mentioned.

Finally, he got a glimpse of a young man and summoned him by his name. 'Where is the room? Didn't I tell you already?' he asked loudly. He couldn't speak in a soft voice. He was used to talking loudly in the fields.

The young man came close and tried to assuage him. He said the bride's family had taken more rooms and only common rooms were available now. 'Please adjust, brother. You could even stay at the wedding hall,' the young man said.

Murugesh was livid. He demanded a separate room and said he was willing to pay. For the young man, it was now a matter of self-respect. He asked Murugesh to wait and left. He told someone that Murugesh was demanding a separate room for himself and his wife.

'Let us leave if we don't get a room,' he told his wife. 'We can pay and find one. I told them repeatedly. How could they do this?'

It appeared all eyes in the wedding hall were on them, as if they were pointing to them, whispering among themselves about how they 'needed a separate room'. It was evident that people were laughing at her.

'The feast is getting over. Eat,' someone said, concerned.

Another said: 'Haven't you eaten yet? The first thing you should do at a wedding is have your meal.' Her hunger was gradually subsiding.

After a while, the young man returned. 'Brother, have your meal. I will arrange a room.'

'No problem. Book a new room for us, I will pay,' Murugesh responded firmly.

'Money is not the issue, brother. It's just that we don't have a room. I will sort it out. Please eat.'

Murugesh took her to the dining hall with a murmur.

She had lost her appetite. His attention was not on the food. His eyes followed the young man and his actions. She finished her meal without raising her head.

The young man was waiting with a key when they came out. They had booked rooms for the groom's friends, and one of them had given theirs up. Murugesh had no patience to listen when the young man sought to explain the great difficulties he had faced in securing the room, and how gracious the friends of the groom had been. He thanked the young man and took the keys. The bride and groom, dressed in modern attire, were at the wedding stage greeting the guests. They could join the guests now and wish the couple.

But Murugesh didn't have the heart. 'Let's do it tomorrow,' he said and left.

The hotel was right opposite the wedding hall. She went to the common room and took her bag. 'Why are you leaving?' a woman asked. She responded with a smile.

He was waiting impatiently. 'Couldn't you have come sooner?' he asked her and walked towards the room allotted to them. She walked behind, head lowered. He locked the room and hugged her waist from behind: 'How hard should I fight for a room?' he asked.

'Get lost,' she said, pushing him away. Throwing herself on the bed, she started crying.

Sandalwood Soap

He couldn't immediately recognize the trembling boy screaming at him: 'Anna! Anna!' The wet floor, the foul smell of the toilets and the young boy clutching his feet felt like something of a conspiracy to upend the regular course of his workday. He thought of all the places he had to visit and the people he had to meet for the day.

Worried, the man slipped his hand into his shirt pocket and picked out a random note. 'Here – ' He tried to give it to the boy.

The boy's tears looked like an attempt to elicit some sympathy, and if they were shed in public, it must be for money, the man thought. Young boys and girls clinging to passengers' feet begging for alms were a common sight on his journeys.

The boy looked up at him, distressed. 'Anna! I am from your home town, Anna,' he said. He started crying harder, and the tears kept flowing.

Shocked, he caught the boy and lifted him up. 'What are you saying?'

'I am Sarasakka's son. Don't you recognize me?'

The boy did look like Sarasakka, come to think of it. 'Come,' he said and took the boy outside.

'Annan is from my home town,' the boy told the man collecting money at the table. It appeared more like he was seeking permission than letting the man know. The money collector said nothing, but gave the boy a strange look.

'Come.' The man gave the boy a push, and walked towards the bus stop.

All his nights dawned at some or the other bus station in the city. The man was familiar with the restrooms of every bus station. Each had different faces: the ones without doors, the ones that appeared like doors, the ones hidden by grates, the ones with rundown doors. He would relieve himself without looking at the unflushed toilet basins. No amount of water could flush them clean. But more irritating than that were the voices that urged him to come out when he had just gone in and managed to lock the door. Every restroom had a person especially for this purpose.

He didn't have the patience to remember their names. He could identify the voices – they were old, middle-aged and childlike. All the voices had the same tone and said the same words. 'Sir, come out. Sir, come out.' The way they knocked on doors was also similar – two quick knocks, as if they were seeking help. The tin doors screeched. The doors would be knocked on again before the screeching stopped.

One or two persons were always waiting at the doors. Even before the door to the stall would open all the way and he would step out, they would splash in a bucket of water. The hand holding the bucket would extend itself, seeking a buck or two. One had to pay twice for the toilet: once here, once at the entrance.

How had the boy gotten into this world? His hand, that had caught hold of the boy, was cold now.

The man had come across many people from his home town on his journeys. The meetings would last as long as a cup of tea. They were an opportunity to reminisce about his past life. He spent most of the day on bus journeys. His job involved meeting reticent people in air-conditioned rooms for a few minutes at a time. Those were official, lifeless meetings. The excitement and happiness of meeting people from his remote village, where even minibuses did not go, was intoxicating for him.

Halfway on their way out of the bus station he looked back at the boy. It looked as if he was struggling hard to put one foot in front of the other. The thin light of the dawn and the sodium lights of the station clearly showed the fatigue in his face.

It was as if he was holding the hand of a replica of Sarasakka, and that made him happy. He thought buying a cup of tea might help the boy, and walked towards the tea shop. The farther they went from the toilet, the better he felt about rescuing the boy from what seemed like grave danger. He felt a sense of adventure in his own step.

He ordered tea and looked for a seat for the boy. The shopkeeper brought around chairs outside the shop. He felt like honouring the shopkeeper with a smile for taking the cue and bringing them the chairs. They were probably his first customers of the day.

The boy had stopped crying and appeared relaxed now. He was dressed in underwear meant for adults. The shirt didn't match it. It was too small for him. His tears had dried up and left tracks on his face. He might be twelve years old – still an innocent child. The man might have seen him as a kid, when Sarasakka was either carrying him on her shoulders, or when walking the toddler on the road.

He stroked the boy's hair softly. He thought it would communicate his love and concern to him.

'Anna – take me away, Anna,' the boy said, his voice laden with sorrow and pain. The boy appeared to hope for some relief through him. It was a demand that would spoil the man's plans for the day. He had to be careful.

'How did you come here, da?'

This small question elicited an elaborate response. He had to intervene often and bring the boy back to the actual story. It appeared that the boy was not willing to finish his story soon: he wanted to spend more time with the man. Why had his day dawned like this? Would this be over any time soon? Where else would this lead him? He felt like he ought to check his daily horoscope.

The boy's story could be summed up in four lines. The family hadn't heard a word from his father who had gone to Kerala for work. While Sarasakka was struggling to raise her kids, a man had come to their village on a bereavement visit. Sarasakka had met him and pleaded with him to employ this boy, her son. 'Please provide him some job or other, and save this family.'

The man had seemed to give it deep thought and generously agreed to take the boy with him. He ran several businesses, which included leasing a huge hotel, a cycle stand and the bus stop toilet. 'Work here for now, I will take you into the hotel later,' the employer had said and sent him off to knock on toilet doors.

The boy told this story in different ways, using various expressions. He lined up evidence in support of his story.

He would give the man tough competition if he took up the man's own job. The inhumanity of having to smell the odour while endlessly flushing the basins full of faeces, the various forms of faeces, the coins thrown at him by those who came out of the toilets – the boy described everything in detail.

Without warning, he showed both his feet. It appeared he had contracted trench foot, having stood in water for long hours. The feet were covered in blisters.

He could only pretend to look at them keenly. If he actually looked at them keenly, he would not be able to leave the boy alone.

After all this, the boy renewed his demand. 'Anna, take me away from here anyhow. It is as if I have shit stuck to my body. I don't even have soap to wash myself. I can't even eat. I feel nauseous. Please take me to my mother.'

He didn't know how to placate the boy. There was no sound except for the two of them drinking tea. Tea helped him guard himself against the boy. But they finished drinking it quickly, even though he tried hard to drink it slowly.

After lighting a cigarette, he felt more at ease. He could now have a casual conversation with the boy.

'When will they send you to the hotel job?'

Sandalwood Soap

'I don't know, Anna. Maybe they don't mean to. Take me to my mother, Anna.'

He had decided what to tell the boy, but took a puff, pretending to think. The boy couldn't handle the silence, and started to speak again.

'They wake me up at three in the morning every day, Anna. From then on, for the entire day, I have to smell the shit. I can't, Anna. Take me away.'

The boy made a barrage of comments along these lines for another minute or two. Each time, he ended it with the same demand: 'Take me away.'

He slowly started to speak his mind.

'Look,' he said. 'I'm working all day today. After this, I have to go to Erode and Coimbatore. It will take me three or four days. I can't go on leave now and take you to our village. I can't take you with me either. Tell me what to do.'

The boy didn't expect the arguments he had kept up for so long to meet such a fate. 'What can we do, Anna?' he asked weakly.

'Shall I tell your employer to send you to work at the hotel?'

The boy immediately rejected the idea. 'He will beat me for letting others know of my plight.'

The man realized that the boy no longer considered him trustworthy. He had suddenly become the 'other'. He couldn't accept that the boy had lost faith in him. He tried to earn back his faith by making him a promise.

'I will pass this place again when coming back from Coimbatore. I will take you then. I will try to send word to your mother if I see someone from our village.'

The boy's face shone with hope and clarity, and he nodded his head. 'Don't worry, I will take you back somehow,' he said reassuringly. He had to say that over and over.

'Okay, Anna,' the boy said, satisfied.

The dawn began to break. A shop – probably a hotel or a lottery shop – played the devotional 'Kaaka Kaaka' song. There was nothing left to say.

'Hang on for two or three days; I will make some arrangements.'

'All right, Anna. You must take me, anyhow. It's already late. They will start scolding me. If I don't pour water for even a little while, the basins will become full and frothy.'

The boy had remembered the place to which he was condemned. He had started to think of the persons there, and the words he would hear. When the boy started walking away, the man suddenly remembered something he had said. He called the boy back and bought him a bar of sandalwood soap. He thought the soap would be an immediate and easy solution to the boy's problems.

Sandalwood Soap

He watched the boy for as long as his smoke lasted. The boy clutched the soap and walked off quickly. Then, work summoned the man.

Certain images kept coming back to the man over the course of the day. The dark-skinned, glowing Sarasakka. Her firm breasts. The mind that warned him about how she was like his sister. The toilet basins that frothed endlessly, even as buckets of water were poured into them. The sandalwood soap in the boy's hands.

More than three months passed. The man had to return to the same city. He remembered the boy when he got down from the bus and walked towards the toilet. Not that he hadn't thought of him before: he had remembered the boy once or twice, in between times. He hadn't had the opportunity to return to his home town. He had felt hesitant to talk about the boy's affairs to people from his home town when he met them by accident. He wondered if he should avoid the toilet and go somewhere else. He didn't have the strength to face the boy.

But his stomach was upset, as usual. The parottas he had eaten mid-journey were doing their job. He couldn't postpone nature's call. He had no choice but to go to the toilet.

He paid the fee, left his bag beneath the table and looked around. The man who was seated across the table was still sleepy.

'Sir, come out. Sir, come out.' He could hear the voices from within the toilet block. None of them sounded like the boy's, but they might be. There were at least one or two persons standing in front of each toilet stall. The person knocking the door was clad in a lungi. It was a relief to imagine that the boy might have left and gone to work at the hotel.

He queued up in front of a stall. Before him was another man waiting for the door to open. The person knocking on the door shouted non-stop: 'Sir, come out! Sir, come out.' When he came closer to the door and knocked, he realized that the lungi-clad person was not an adult. He was the boy. A faded, ordinary lungi had changed his appearance.

He was hesitant to talk to the boy. It would be better to use the toilet and leave without letting the boy know. A voice, deep down, said softly that that would be unfair. He decided to heed the voice.

The boy, meanwhile, had gone to the other corner of the queue, carrying a small bucket filled with water. He didn't want to summon the boy by clapping his hands. He hadn't asked the boy his name when they had met last time. He felt bad about his lack of concern in not even asking for a name despite their long conversation. Even if he had known his name, he didn't think it was possible to use it at this place.

Sandalwood Soap

He waited for the boy to come back.

It didn't look like the door he was standing in front of was going to open any time soon. There was another man waiting before him. Each door had at least two people waiting. People kept coming in, looking for queues to join. The boy's voice didn't shake up anyone inside.

A door screeched open with a big sound. A man emerged from a toilet in the middle, holding his dhoti up. He looked like the sort of man who would spend a long time in the toilets. The boy came running to the door and splashed the bucket of water inside. No one knew if the water fell inside the toilet or outside.

The boy extended his hand to the man. His stomach was now relieved, so he didn't fuss much and handed a coin to the boy. The boy was doing a service, after all.

The boy drew closer to his side. His hands knocked on the door as he kept up the refrain: 'Sir, come out.'

The man stretched a bit and touched the boy's shoulder.

'Don't hurry, sir. They will come out soon, please wait,' the boy said, then looked at him and immediately identified him. 'Anna, is that you? When did you come?' He was embarrassed by the boy's surprise and his welcoming tone.

The man standing in front of him turned and smiled faintly. The boy didn't respond.

'Anna, wait!' he said and ran to knock on the doors

again. 'Come out, sir.' The words carried a tone of fatigue and command.

It appeared that one door would open soon. The boy stood next to it and called him, 'Anna, come, Anna, come here.'

He couldn't decide whether he had to go or not. Everyone was looking at him. 'Come, Anna, quick,' the boy said. A man emerged, his pants rolled up, from that toilet. He avoided all the eyes by heeding only the boy's voice. His stomach was forcing him to do so too. He walked towards the boy.

'Preferential treatment even for this,' someone murmured. He heard that loud and clear. He hung his head, and didn't look at those waiting before the door. The boy splashed the water carefully this time. The man went into the toilet and locked the door. Until he unlocked the door, there were no knocks, no voices urging him to come out. He was able to empty his stomach in peace. But he was ashamed of the boy's favour for him.

The boy was waiting to welcome him back when he stepped out of the toilet. Placing the bucket on the water tank, the boy held his hands: 'Come, Anna.' He didn't even think of rolling down his pants, and continued to feel too ashamed to look at others as he stepped out with the boy.

'Annan is from my home town. I am going with him for a bit,' the boy told the man collecting the money.

'Where are you going when there's such a rush?' the man sneered.

Unfazed, the boy responded firmly: 'I will be back.'

The boy carried the man's bag and walked out, the lungi flowing past his legs. He held the bag in one hand and the corner of the lungi in the other. The man didn't know what to say to the boy. He thought about how he had not returned to their home town, about how he hadn't sent word to the boy's mother nor returned as promised. He walked beside him, full of guilt.

It was dawn and the boy was brisk.

'Listen to him, like he's a big somebody, as if he's seen the crowd himself,' the boy scoffed about the money collector.

The man was afraid the boy would ask him questions, but the boy chattered on about the place and its people. He could not comprehend his talk fully. He took the boy to a tea shop and ordered tea.

'How long will you be here, Anna?' the boy asked.

'Just today. I'll leave as soon as the job's over.'

He wanted to update the boy before he could ask him anything. 'I couldn't go home, da.'

The boy smiled. 'Must've been difficult. I know.'

It was very comforting. He hoped that the conversation about this wouldn't last any longer, and it turned out to be that way. After tea, the boy said: 'Anna, come whenever you are here. I will be around.'

He suddenly seemed to remember something and reached into the pocket of his underwear beneath the lungi. After much effort, he pulled them out – crumpled hundred-rupee notes.

'Five hundred rupees. My earnings, apart from the salary. I don't know whether you will go in person or send it through someone. Please give it to my mother.'

The man took the money with utmost respect.

'It'll take another two or three months for me to come home. Please tell my mother I will bring my salary myself then.'

The man nodded his head.

'Please don't tell my mother that I work in the toilets, Anna.' The boy's voice was subdued and face sad when he made this request. 'I won't,' the man promised.

'All right, Anna. It's getting late. I have to go. Don't leave without meeting me whenever you're here,' the boy said. He started to walk away under the lights. From a few steps off, he turned and said in a raised voice: 'I still use the sandalwood soap that you bought for me. It smells good.'

It looked like there was a faint smile on his face.

Hail, Comrade PM!

Comrade PM was nowhere in sight when I awoke. The rays of the sun fell sharply on my face, as if mocking me for sleeping late. The thatched roof reminded me of where I was. What would Comrade PM have thought of me? That I was a lazy and irresponsible fellow? On some future occasion he would probably level this opinion at me as a criticism.

I hadn't slept well the previous night; the place was new to me. It was only near dawn that I fell asleep and slept like a log. But what would people here think if I slept in at a strange place? This was where the workers lived. Comrade PM had already warned me, too, that this was peanut harvesting season. People went off to the fields before dawn while it was still dark.

Nobody would have noticed that I have slept so long, I told myself.

Where might this Comrade PM have gone? He could have told me, or taken me along. Why had he abandoned me at this new place?

I happened to be lying in a thatched shed with no doors. Opposite was a small thatched hut that had walls for the sake of it. I stood at the entrance between the shed and the hut, stretched my hands, yawned and looked around. There was not one human around. All I could hear were thin, unintelligible voices from afar. A single crow cawed from somewhere. I didn't know what to do.

The buffalo calf tied to a neem tree raised its head and looked at me. Its eyes were filled with fear. It trotted about the tree, bleating. What kind of comradeship is it to abandon a person new to some place? Comrade PM had brought me to an area with no electricity no less. I had no idea what this place was like.

I was upset with him and used a cuss word or two for him to myself.

My eyes were getting used to the light of the sun. From one angle, it shone like a halo. I went inside and sat back on the cot. The blanket I had been given lay crumpled in the middle. I folded it. Looking around, I caught sight of a water pot, bent slightly out of shape. A mild breeze created ripples in the water inside the pot. The ripples looked inviting. I gargled and washed my face with the water. Its chill brought about clarity in my heart. I would feel better if I drank some.

The thatch door was shut firmly with the help of a stick. I was embarrassed to open it to drink water. The family were supporters of the party, yet it was not right to go inside the house when no one was around. The water I had used to gargle would have to do. I collected some water in both my hands and drank it. The moss underneath the pot was rippling now. The water shrank my stomach, which realized that it had been empty for a while.

There were dogs lying about on the uneven lanes of the street. It looked like all the houses were empty. To my surprise, everyone, from the children to the elders, had gone to the fields. I was the only person in the midst of forty or fifty huts. Had Comrade PM gone to work with them? Whatever the case, shouldn't he have told me?

I squatted on a lane near the shed and pissed in a hurry, afraid that I would be caught by someone approaching from some unseen corner, and stood up. The buffalo calf stood at the opposite edge of the stake to which it was tethered. I didn't know how to give it hope.

Let Comrade PM come when he would. I decided to take a stroll and look for a tea shop.

I put on the shirt that was hanging on a pole in the shed. A bed sheet and a thick book lay on the cot used by Comrade PM. I had a vain hope that the book might hold a letter for me from Comrade PM, some message of sorts. It was Lenin's *What Is to Be Done?* The book had only Lenin's words and no note from Comrade PM as I had hoped. But then, he wouldn't have gone far. Maybe he had had a message to pass on to the comrades. It could be a local chore, which he would quickly finish and come back. The book gave me hope that he would be back soon.

I felt at peace and went looking for a tea shop.

Comrade PM had brought me to this place late last night. I knew nothing about its residential areas. In the dark, I had simply understood that we were walking among the huts, all of which looked nearly alike. A cow or a buffalo calf stood next to almost every hut. In many places, there were tracks left by goat dung. It was a slum colony, occupied by the working class. The party had worked hard to build a structure in these areas. Ordinary citizens now used terms like 'comrade' casually.

The mobilization had been so strong that the party believed that this area would be the epicentre of revolution in the future. So, newer comrades like me were sent to these areas to feel optimistic about party activities and to be trained in party work among the people. As I had been in the party for over a year, they decided to elevate me from a supporter and move me to the next level. I was asked to spend my holidays in this area as part of this process. I had romantic ideas about villages and villagers, and so had no qualms about coming here.

I saw open fields soon after I emerged from the huts. A single lane ran through the fields. I thought I might find a tea shop if I walked through the lane. I had no doubt that all roads led to tea shops. However remote a village is, a tea shop still serves as a place that brings the village together. I walked hopefully down the lane.

How would Comrade PM, who had abandoned me without even guiding me to a tea shop, guide the people towards revolution? The party might have made a wrong choice with him. I could not explain the abhorrence I felt for Comrade PM. It might perhaps have mellowed down if I had been able to find a tea shop soon. But the single lane passed from one field to another, and a tea shop was still nowhere in sight.

It was certain that all the curves would eventually lead to a big road. When we reached here last night, we had got out of the bus at this very place and entered this path. So I continued to walk, unfazed. I had real tea cravings now. It was getting hotter. When I wandered into the maize fields, I unexpectedly ran into Comrade PM.

I felt very relieved to see him. 'What is this, Comrade? You have abandoned me,' I yelled, a livid expression on my face. I tried to pin blame on him, but Comrade PM remained cool and smiled. What a divine smile it was.

'Got scared?' he asked.

'Not so. But there was no human being around. The calves were staring at me. I was helpless. Where did you disappear to?'

'Didn't I tell you before that this is peanut harvesting season? People leave at dawn for work. It's the only way they can harvest enough. It is difficult when it's hot.'

Comrade PM went on to explain the intricacies of harvesting peanuts. Worried that he would start talking about people and their livelihoods, I cut in. 'Fine, come. Let's take a stroll and have some tea.'

I realized that he had said a lot but hadn't yet revealed where he had gone. I assumed it was on some secret mission. He stood still before me, deep in contemplation, and I stood looking over his shoulder. I hoped the comrade would take me to a tea shop.

He said, 'We have to walk a long distance to a tea shop. Let's not. We will go back.' He walked back towards the colony, bypassing me. What kind of mobilization was he going to do when there were no people there?

'Comrade, I need to drink tea to feel better,' I said.

He must have been surprised at how stubborn I was. 'How can you be hankering after tea, Comrade?' he asked.

Hail, Comrade PM!

I had no other choice but to explain my predicament to him. I told him how I was so accustomed to drinking tea every day and how it affected my day if I missed it. Finally, I said it clearly, 'I cannot perform my ablutions if I don't drink tea.'

'Are you talking about taking a shit?' he asked.

'Yes, Comrade. I can empty my bowels only after I drink something hot. My stomach's bond with tea is deep.' I smiled sheepishly.

Comrade PM gave deep thought to my predicament. He stroked his greying beard. He was not part of a state-level committee, but I was certain that Comrade PM was an important figure in the district-level committee. I had placed my demand before him. It was up to him to find a solution. Both parties were cognizant of the issue. All that was left was to debate it.

Comrade PM's words opened the argument. 'What is to be done, Comrade?' he asked.

What could I tell him? How would he react if I suggested that we both break off the argument and wade into the field across us, to toil over the maize crop? I decided to stick to my position.

'Let's go have some tea, Comrade,' I told him.

He broke off a small twig from a neem plant, removed the leaves and handed half of it to me. He spoke while sharpening the edge of the twig. 'This is the demonstration of a petit-bourgeois mindset in you, Comrade. What would ordinary people do if they had to drink tea every morning as soon as they woke up? Can they afford to buy tea powder, milk and sugar? Your lifestyle should change, Comrade. You should quit the bourgeois attitude and live and work with the working class. If one can take a shit only after drinking tea, lakhs of people in this country will have to live without taking a shit.'

He stopped his lecture abruptly, possibly after noticing the changes in my expression. His voice toned down a bit and he declared, 'These are all mere habits, Comrade. Try not drinking tea today. Let's see whether you can take a shit or not.'

My stomach was churning. It was most certainly not related to my bowel movements. It was because of missing out on tea. I stopped short of telling him that we could debate this after we had drunk some. Whatever the case, Comrade PM was a senior and a man of experience – an intellectual, even.

I didn't know how to nudge him towards a glass of tea. He walked over the fields, but not towards the colony. We came across a stream amidst thorny bushes. My tongue couldn't handle the bitterness of the neem twig, and I kept spitting as I walked. 'Only the haves form habits. What will the have-nots do? The habit ought to be not to drink. The party has given you this opportunity to quit this petit-bourgeois mindset that you have. You should use it.'

I felt embarrassed by his repeated mention of the petit-bourgeois mindset. It stopped me from arguing further. Very irritated, I cleared my throat, spat again and tried to add force to my point. 'The oppressed also drink tea, Comrade. I have seen that in their neighbourhoods. There are many people who take a bowl and go to a tea shop as soon as they wake up in the mornings.'

He was probably hoping for this response. He was happy that I had joined the debate. My response facilitated a response in turn. He continued, 'Why do oppressed people take a bowl and go to tea shops, Comrade? Because they can skip a meal if they drink tea. The tea helps to handle their hunger. If they could afford a meal for the same price, would they choose tea?' he asked.

He had clarified an especially important point for me, striking me dumb. I looked at him silently. He understood that he had laid a strong foundation, going by my silence, and decided to build on it.

'I don't deny that the oppressed drink tea. Do you know the tricks played by estate owners to make people drink tea? When they want to boost their sales, they try to draw in people from every stratum of society as consumers of tea. The oppressed are no exception. It is just that they get the worst quality of tea. The profit from every glass of tea consumed by an ordinary human in this society goes to the estate owners, Comrade.'

The argument put forth by Comrade PM gave a sense of universality to a small issue. I stood before him helplessly, unable to come up with an argument justifying tea-drinking. When I started to think, the comrade tried to nip my bourgeois mindset in the bud. He continued with his arguments, and raised several questions.

I listened patiently, and finally said, sadly, 'Fine, Comrade. I will drink tea just for today.'

He was shocked that I hadn't changed my mind despite his arguments. He decided to convince me with actions, having failed to do so with words and arguments. 'Look here, Comrade. *Don't* drink tea just for today. Let's see whether you take a shit or not. If you don't, I will buy you tea tomorrow.'

The look of self-pity on my face made him soften further. He gave me more concessions. 'Not even for a day, Comrade. Let's wait until evening. If you can't take a shit, I will buy you tea.'

Comrade PM had levelled an appropriate punishment for my petit-bourgeois mentality on the first day of my visit here. I found his decision acceptable. I was hopeful of drinking tea in the evening.

We entered the neighbourhood again. I was not in the best of spirits. Maybe I shouldn't have come to the party training at all. If I couldn't control myself for a glass of tea, would I be able to make bigger sacrifices needed for a revolution? I feared my emotional sincerity was not adequate. The comrade's test might be the first effort to move me to the next level. If I passed this test, the comrade might direct me to not drink tea ever. I was confused. I thought about it over and over, and a debate raged in my mind. *Proposition: What should be the priority in life – Party or Tea? Or perhaps: Revolution or Tea?* My heart was inclined to tea, but how could I not stand by the revolution? If I decided I needed both in my life, Comrade PM would ask me thus, 'So, you treat tea and revolution alike?' What could I tell him?

I walked on without uttering a word. The comrade walked beside me, silent himself. He probably wanted to leave me alone with my thoughts.

We reached the old house where I had fallen asleep. We gargled and washed our faces. The comrade opened the thatched door, went in and came back with two vessels of fermented rice and water. The fermented rice cooled my burning stomach. The rice was aromatic, and not too sour. A piece of onion or pickle would have enhanced the taste further. The thought probably occurred to Comrade PM too.

'See this, Comrade. These people cannot even afford a pickle to go with this meal. Try telling them that they can take a shit only if they drink tea. They would laugh at you.'

I grinned sheepishly again. What else could I do? He said, further, 'I have seen people who say they can only take a shit if they drink tea or have a smoke. It is merely an excuse to drink tea or have a smoke.'

'Is that so?' I asked.

'Of course, Comrade. We become addicted to habits. So, the mind misleads us to think so.'

Comrade PM was approaching the issue psychologically. The fermented rice made me sleepy. I lay on the cot. Comrade PM sat on another cot and opened a book.

'Wait a while, Comrade,' he said. 'Whatever is inside has to come out, right?'

Whatever is inside would come out, obviously. How had I missed this logic? It was clear that Comrade PM had vowed to relieve me of my petit-bourgeois mentality in a single day by doing away with my tea-drinking.

I was fatigued. I assumed it was because I hadn't drunk my dose of tea. Comrade PM would leave in a while. He

Hail, Comrade PM!

had to have many tasks lined up. After he left, I thought I would step out to find a tea shop. Who knew? The party supporter living in this house might well be a tea drinker. They would probably have tea or coffee powder here. I could make myself some black coffee.

It would help if Comrade PM went away. I tried to investigate. 'Do you have somewhere to be, Comrade?'

As if sensing my plans, he said with a smile, 'No, Comrade. The people must return this evening after work. I have to meet and talk to them. That's the only work I have. Until then, I will read and take notes. Do you want something to read? There are some books.' He looked into his bag.

'Not now, Comrade. I will read later.' I was relieved that he didn't insist further. I closed my eyes. My focus returned to my stomach. Was anything happening after the meal? There was no pain in the stomach. The food should have put pressure on my bowels. But my stomach belied the logic and remained hard. It also looked slightly bloated. I couldn't belch, either. My body was dull. I didn't feel like moving my hands or feet. My head was heavy like a stone. Somehow, I fell asleep.

When I woke up again, the sun was blazing, and I was sweating profusely. I looked at Comrade PM. He remained as he had been, seated with a book open. I felt guilty that I had fallen asleep while he was reading. Noticing me awaken, Comrade PM asked, 'Anything happening, Comrade?'

I gave it a thought. The stomach looked as it had when I had gone to sleep. But I pretended that it was now soft.

I could if I try, I told myself. I could not let the comrade feel hopeless. He would start talking about how hope was important in life. I told him, 'Looks like something is happening, Comrade.'

Comrade PM was excited. His face was bright. He took a glass of water from underneath the cot. 'Drink this, Comrade,' he said. I finished half of it, being thirsty anyway. The comrade encouraged me to drink more. I couldn't. It was nauseating. 'Enough, Comrade,' I told him. The pleading tone of my voice stopped him from forcing me any further.

'Let's walk for a bit, come,' he said.

We walked slowly. Comrade PM didn't say a word about tea. He probably didn't want to remind me of it. He spoke happily about other things. His conversation was about the people of this area and how to mobilize them as a party organization. Chancing upon a pit filled with seemai karuvelam thorns, Comrade PM stopped and told me, 'Hide yourself, Comrade. Keep your stomach loose. Be normal, be relaxed. You can do this.'

Hail, Comrade PM!

I ventured into the pit, with his words for support. I could feel the water moving in my stomach. I sat at a place covered by thick thorns. I couldn't see Comrade PM from there. It felt like I was enclosed within four walls. *My stomach is giving in,* I thought. I controlled my breath and tried harder.

Finally, Comrade PM achieved some degree of success.

Magamuni

Velaatha's feet twirled and swayed. There were no feet like hers to be found anywhere in the sprawling courtyard of the loom mill whose entire space was occupied by the force of the feet that ran on the looms. Velaatha's feet chased those standing in the way to the corners of the walls. Her hands, raised above her head, were knotted together like a garland. Her eyes were closed. The border of her sari, wound tightly, didn't move at all. Her feet, which measured the floor with each movement, were forceful and robust. No sound could be heard, except for her breaths. Like an animal resting after hours hunting a large prey, she knelt on the floor, her head still spinning. The feet beneath the bended knees were still twirling. The rough concrete floor did no harm to her knees.

Everyone stood around, their hands folded as a mark of respect. She often stared at those who seemed indifferent.

She sighed at them. Her feet twirled in their direction. People were awed by the strength in those frail-looking feet. When she knelt and twirled in a snake dance, her hair came unbound, flowing over her back.

The tresses that flowed past her waist made many patterns as she danced. They fell to the left after a particular move. In another unexpected moment, she sharply crooked her neck, lifting her hair. It fell to the front, covering her face. She danced for a long time with her face covered. Many pairs of eyes were fixed on her bare back.

Her body was at ease with the movements of the dance now. The hands raised above her head remained firm. She was unanswerable: no one there could keep their own hands folded for very long. The employer stood with utmost respect, a towel wrapped around his waist. The pictures of the gods were lined up, waiting to be worshipped. Velaatha's dance showed no sign of stopping.

The supervisor picked up the puja plate and stood in front of her. Her dance was getting fierce. He put some sacred ash on her head. After she was smeared with it three times, she let out a violent sound, unfurling her hands and stretching them wide. The supervisor gave her some of the sacred ash. She refused and demanded something else. He didn't quite understand.

Someone else brought a tablet of camphor, placed it on her hand and lit it. She stared as it burned. Her face shone red from the light of the flame. When the camphor burned brightest, she opened her mouth and swallowed it in a state of frenzy. Then she fell on the floor. Her tresses covered her like a blanket. She did not wake even after the puja ritual was over and the prasadam had been distributed. No one interfered with her, either.

The trances had been going on for months and had started on a Friday. That day had been less frenzied. It was the supervisor's habit to burn incense and wave it around the mill. He would do this for all the eighty looms there, and it would take at least fifteen minutes for him to finish this rite. Status quo had to be maintained at every loom until he returned. Only after his return would camphor be burnt, and the worship rituals held.

It was during this interval that Velaatha's head reeled like she was in a stupor because of the smell of the incense. She never moved an inch from where she stood, yet her head reeled.

Soon, all eyes were on her. People scoffed and murmured. Her eyes were closed, and she saw nothing. Her head turned swiftly when the camphor was lit, and shook again.

Velaatha soon became a topic of discussion among

people working both shifts at the mill. It was widely believed that she was haunted by Mohini, the one who resided in the very centre of the mill, who strutted around in the middle of the night, making a loud noise with her anklets. They said Mohini had devised this plot to attract young men and gently warned one another not to fall prey to her. There was another belief: that Velaatha was haunted by her own husband who had left her a month or two after their wedding, never to return. He had possibly died like an orphan somewhere else and was now haunting his wife. 'He couldn't control her when he was a human. Let him do it as a ghost,' some laughed.

A few suspected that she could be haunted by Ottukaatu Magamuni, who was also called Aatur Kaaliyamman. Others disagreed. She was not pure enough to be possessed by the gods. Ghosts practised deception by appearing as gods, some said. The priest from the Keezhkaatu temple vouched for these naysayers.

Whether or not Velaatha paid heed to any of those words, she responded to none. She spoke very little. It seemed like she had lost hope in language, but kept her smile intact to give to those who crossed her path. When she had to speak out of necessity, she didn't utter more than a word or two.

'For two days,' Velaatha had said when she had to

cross a temporary bridge being built across a lake. On the second day, a flood washed the bridge away, leaving no trace of it. From then on, they intently listened to her every word, assuming it had a message for them. When she didn't speak, they made every effort to extract a word from her.

Velaatha took about half an hour of the Friday pujas every week, without fail. Week after week, her dance grew more disciplined. She didn't particularly focus on mastering the steps, mobilizing the scattered crowd or bringing the floor alive. But they occurred spontaneously.

They made efforts to discover who possessed her, or get some word out of her. They lit camphor, prostrated before her and asked her questions. She responded to no one. No word issued from her except for the sounds she made when dancing. Within weeks, they were tired. They even began to talk of her deceiving them. That talk, too, died down soon.

It was neither Friday nor evening. It was past noon in the middle of the week. Velaatha became possessed when winding a pirn. She started twirling amidst the sounds of the looms. They stopped the machines, worried that she would fall into one of them when they were in operation. The looms were never stopped except for occasions like Diwali or Pongal. The mill owner came running when the noise stopped: he had built his house on the top of the mill and was attuned to the sound of the looms.

Velaatha's dance was at its peak when he came down. She danced among the looms without colliding with them. This was embarrassing for the mill owner and an unprecedented crisis. It had been embarrassing ever since she had started the dances. He could no longer chide her as usual and felt like he was committing a mistake when he called her in alone. He had to give her money when she came asking for it. He couldn't even admonish her when she took a day off without informing him.

Now this was going to impede the day's work, too. They brought in the camphor plate, hoping to ward off the spirit sooner. They flung the sacred ash at her and tried to place camphor on her hand.

She bit her tongue and let out a ferocious cry, something she had never done before. Her fragile body couldn't handle the ferocity of this possession. Some bystanders felt pity for her. Her hand did not extend to receive the camphor. Instead, she stood in the heart of the mill, raised her head and hands, and shook from head to toe, as if readying to make a statement.

In a slender voice of a bird emerging out of a cave, she said: 'An evil is approaching.'

'What evil has befallen us, Saami?' the owner asked, falling at her feet.

Now her voice was forceful. 'An evil is approaching,' she said again, this time with more clarity.

Pavalayi, a worker in the mill, whispered something into the ear of the owner. The owner now said: 'Whatever the evil, Saami, you should help us tide over.'

She said, 'Hmmm,' as if considering his prayer. He repeated his request and fell at her feet again.

'What will you do for Magamuni?'

The question left the entire mill shocked and unnerved. They realized that it was Magamuni who possessed her. 'Magamuni herself!' they said and fell at her feet.

'I will sacrifice a goat and make pongal offerings, Saami,' the owner said. The god now extended its hand as if ready to leave. It swallowed the camphor, satiated its thirst and left.

Later in the afternoon, people realized what the 'evil' was. The mill owner also had several lorries. One of them, driven by his own son, had met with an accident. The son was unhurt, but the lorry was slightly damaged. The owner was dumbstruck when he was informed of this over the phone.

When he did speak, 'Magamunipa' was the first word he uttered. He hadn't quite been convinced even when the god had made her demand. But now, his devotion for Magamuni and respect for Velaatha went up. Was it any ordinary thing to save his son? He vowed to sacrifice two goats and offer two pongals, and rushed to Velaatha to fall at her feet.

The news spread like wildfire.

People came to get prophecies from Velaatha. But she didn't utter a word to anyone, responding only with a smile. They were disappointed, but maintained their respect for her. Her dances on Fridays continued like before. Aside from those who worked in the mill, outsiders began to turn up to witness it, too. The owner had to spend more to ensure there was enough prasadam for every Friday visitor, but he was happy to do it.

The crowds started dwindling when their expectations were belied, and Magamuni made no prophecies. But Velaatha continued to enjoy the same respect in the town.

Only the priest from Keezhkaatu refused to trust Velaatha, and spoke against her everywhere. 'Doesn't a person require some standards to be possessed?' was his question. 'Would Magamuni descend on a cheap woman like her?' he was heard saying at dawn in a tea shop.

He was happy that she hadn't gotten into the soothsaying

business, but he was worried that her popularity and the respect she commanded would affect his own prospects. He had chased away innumerable demons. Many were the spirits confined to the tamarind trees lining the roads, subdued by his whip. He couldn't perform the way he used to, but some people still came looking for him.

It could not be called a professional rivalry, but he was worried that she would walk away with the respect due to him. The tone and tenor of his voice changed with each passing day. 'She's possessed by an evil spirit,' he said with conviction. 'I will chase it away,' he said with a sense of pride.

One such declaration led to an intense debate in the tea shop. 'Can you prove that she's possessed by an evil spirit rather than a god?' they asked him. He took it as a challenge, and said he would prove it the following Friday.

The news spread everywhere and reached Velaatha's ears. She responded with her usual smile.

Next Friday, the entire town gathered for the puja at the mill. Velaatha's head started to shake the moment the incense started burning. The priest was not present at that moment, but just as people thought that he had given up, he made an appearance.

He ventured into Velaatha's territory, a towel tied across his waist and ash smeared on his forehead. People laughed and egged him on, as if sending a wrestler to a bout. Eyes closed, lost in her dance, Velaatha's dancing feet crossed the whole mill. The floor shook with her movements, and every pair of legs started to tremble. When her hair came loose and fanned over her back, and by her dance after that happened, the priest was convinced that she was possessed by an evil spirit. He did not, however, say so out loud.

He murmured to himself and folded his hands. Then he fell to the floor, paid his respects and stood up. His voice was clearly heard by everyone in the mill. 'Saami Magamunipa! We are happy that you've come. I have chased many evil spirits away with your blessings. Ghosts also deceive us by pretending to be gods. You should clarify if it is indeed you, or a ghost.' It was not evident that he was speaking directly to Velaatha. His gaze as he spoke was directed to the space at large. He seemed not to be making any specific address.

Velaatha stretched her hands and let out a sound.

He continued, 'I have something on my mind. Only you can discover what it is. If you do so, my doubts will be clarified. You should say it before the camphor is lit and the lamps shown. Saami Appa! Magamuni!'

He folded his hands and stepped back. How long would it take for Magamuni to announce what was in the priest's mind? Would Magamuni spare him if he contradicted her utterance? The crowd was keen to know the end. They knew that the thing the priest had in mind would decide the outcome of this battle. Some among them were secretly happy about the crisis that Velaatha had to face.

Velaatha continued her fierce dance. She stretched her hands to the front, something she had not done in the past. It was as if she were holding a whip. Her sari looked as if it would come off her any time. The dance continued until the camphor was lit. No word was uttered.

Then suddenly, she screamed: 'Dei!' The sound of her gnashing teeth was loud, reverberating across the mill.

'Are you testing me?' she asked and paused. Silent faces all around. Waiting for her word.

She sighed heavily and then said, 'She lives far away from your field, to the east. A widow. You are thinking of her, da,' she said. The *da* was particularly violent.

The god was ready to leave. Everyone smiled and looked around for the priest, but he had disappeared in a trice.

The Last Cloth

His mother's breasts were the problem. *Shamelessly barbaric*, he censured her in his mind. When he woke up, long after the risen sun had flung its rays over the world, and sat on the veranda brushing his teeth, she would be rambling about, picking fodder for the cattle or carrying cow dung on her head. The border of her sari, that flowed from her waist to the knees, would be tied up neatly over her back and draped over her head, to help carry the dung basket.

Her sagging breasts moved like small knives meant to cut dried palms. The movement troubled him. He could barely sit in front of her. She was unaffected by her wrinkled breasts, as if they didn't exist. That troubled him even more, and he hated her even more. He was ashamed that these breasts had nurtured him with their milk. He was hugely embarrassed by the thought that he was born from her bleeding vagina. It would be better if she hid her breasts, at least when he was around.

He tried to communicate this through various gestures, like turning his face away or lowering his head. She didn't seem to understand, though.

He would run away to the fields or to the well to avoid those breasts. But his mother would follow, looking for him to run an errand. The breasts devoured the glowing love in her face and danced. Nervous and sweating, he would vow to cut them off with a long sword. He could think only of leaving the place anyhow, immediately.

Even if he went into the thatched shed on the terrace meant for him, he would still tremble nervously. He felt better only after lying on his stomach and closing his eyes. He would refuse to come down to eat when he heard his mother's voice. The dancing breasts were like weird animals. They hit him when she served him food. He couldn't avoid them, no matter how hard he tried. He only wanted to wash his hands as quickly as possible and go back up to his room.

He had been home from his studies for a month, and he never wanted to go out again. He was worried about facing questions about his mother and her breasts. He thought people would make fun of her breasts and laugh behind his back. Worried that the question could come up from anyone about his mother and her breasts, he would constantly think about leaving every conversation as soon as he could. He would read through the pages of huge books as if looking for solutions in the medicine he had studied. But eventually, he would get tired and nod off.

He was ashamed to set foot outside the door. How could he go anywhere before he had decided how to handle his mother if she crossed his path?

He wondered if he could talk to his brother's wife about it. But what could he tell her? The words would almost surface before he retracted them and let them die. He was hopeful that his sister-in-law would understand. The trouble was with initiating the conversation. He struggled with it like a newcomer in a foreign country. He would try to talk about it during mealtimes now and then, but he just ate without raising his head and left. His nights were a struggle, too. Was he alone in having such a mother? he would ask the lizards.

They would ignore him, keen on capturing insects.

There was nothing wrong with his mother's health. There was no dearth in her love. But the breasts were so exposed.

He wondered if he should cut all ties and run away.

Were these the breasts that nurtured and nourished him, that had helped him towards the crowning achievement of his degree? Why did this have to happen to him?

A theatre owner, the father of a beautiful girl, came around to get his daughter married to him, promising to build him a hospital. That made the problem worse. He didn't want a stranger to see his mother. When they sent word about their visit to see the groom, the entire house was overjoyed, thrilled about his stroke of good luck. When his sister-in-law sought to remove the look of worry from his face, he gathered just enough courage to splutter:

'Amma's breasts ...'

Was that all, the sister-in-law wondered. Yet she saw an opportunity. Here was a family problem that she could sort out. She worried about her mother-in-law's breasts, too. When she spoke of her brother-in-law, in glowing terms, it turned out that everyone had similar thoughts. They all acknowledged his problem.

The sister-in-law came up with quite a simple solution that earned everyone's praise.

'We will stitch a blouse for Athai before they come to see the groom.'

They were relieved. They believed that a problem that lived among them all along was suddenly coming to a quick end. A single voice ran through the fields, the cattle sheds and everywhere: 'We could get a blouse stitched.'

Nobody thought it necessary to find out his mother's opinion about a blouse. Everyone was seized by the happiness and pride of setting right a long-perpetuated wrong. They smiled sheepishly when they spoke of a blouse to her. They hoped she would be as excited as they were and show it in words if not in gestures.

But she was stunned. She was speechless. It was as if a strange hand were groping her all over as soon as she was told about stitching a blouse. No one cared about the sorry state of her face, which looked like land untouched by a plough. They genuinely thought that the idea would make her happy.

She stroked her breasts, sagging from the fatigue of nourishing children. The breasts touched her stomach, tired and unaware of the others' plans. They had been growing like fresh coconut saplings when she had just attained puberty. They were full and glowing sensuously when her husband ran his tongue over them the night after their wedding, burying his head between them. The children who suckled her breasts as she walked, carrying them along, and the significance of her breasts at those times – she thought about them all.

She could not remember anyone thinking or talking

about covering them with a scrap of a blouse. The border of her sari ran like a straight line across her body and sometimes didn't cover her fully.

She could not fully comprehend their idea of giving her something that was denied to her in her prime.

Her eldest daughter-in-law was happily busy with the wedding chores, as if the brother-in-law with a medical qualification were getting married to a foreign bride. She was also in charge of the blouse issue. She wanted to try out her old blouse on her athai for measurements. When her athai frowned as if the blouse had a bad odour, she thought, *Look at the arrogance of this old woman!*

She vowed to adorn her mother-in-law with a blouse. But when the blouse in her hand brushed across her mother-in-law, the cloth made a sound like the screech of a myna, and impeded the task.

The mother-in-law cried as if she was experiencing a pain that no labour had caused her. All movements stopped except for that sound. She gathered all her strength to control the pain. However hard she tried, she couldn't raise her hand fully. Flabbergasted, the daughter-in-law stepped back, still in a state of fear.

What can an old woman do? she told herself.

The household was excited on the day they decided to buy the blouse. Nobody had any inhibitions talking about it. Her doctor son laughed to himself. Had he really been worried about something to which everyone had so easily agreed? His dreams were no longer about shrivelled breasts. He was no longer afraid of seeing his mother. In his mind, she was clad in a blouse. The image of the sagging breasts exposing themselves had ceased to trouble him.

He spent his time dreaming about his wedding, about his future as a doctor in his hospital building. He joined his sister-in-law for the wedding shopping. They had to travel thirty kilometres to the city to buy things, so about ten or fifteen people woke at dawn and left for the city.

The mother remained in the empty house, deep in pain.

It was certain that she would have to wear a blouse. How could she walk about as she was now? Could she walk at all? She wondered if she could take care of the goats and the cattle any more. Would they know her if her breasts were covered? She imagined the blouse piece as a small knife that would cut off all her movements. She wondered how it would feel on her breasts.

The house was so deserted that even birds didn't pass by. She was too immersed in her thoughts to do any work.

When they came home in the afternoon, their bodies burnt in the sun, they were shocked to see her state. The tumour, just showing up, covered her cleavage. The doctor son rushed to his room for his new stethoscope and examined her. Everybody was nervous, worried that the purchase of the blouse would end up being a futile exercise. He was shaken by the thought of having to touch his mother after a long while. He turned his eyes from the breasts.

Smiling at the frightened faces, he said: 'This is an ordinary tumour, easily removed. Even if it can't be, the blouse will cover this up, too.'

Everyone was happy at the mention of the blouse. They talked incessantly about how big the shop was and how many varieties of blouses there were. She heard them all, but also noticed that no one was carrying a blouse piece.

It turned out that they had bought not one piece, but a dozen. At least six of those shone like a snake's skin. They were meant to be worn when stepping out. The doctor son said the material was the product of an English-speaking nation that ruled the world. Another six were made of domestic cloth, meant to be worn at home. Her breasts were to be covered all the time, everywhere. They had made all the arrangements. The tailors stitching the blouses were well known, too. They had ten people merely to note the measurements.

Many were jealous that the old woman would wear blouses stitched by reputed tailors.

The Last Cloth

She stopped working altogether after hearing the news about blouses getting made, and the tumour covered her cleavage. She couldn't raise her hands high enough. What difference would it make, anyway? It was a couple of days' struggle to adjust.

The family decided to sell the goats at the market and keep only a minimum number of cattle.

She couldn't imagine life without the sounds of her goats bleating. She would roam the fields and the lands. She passed the time watching a stranger graze his goats. She felt that her life hinged on their bleating sounds. Amid the khirni and neem trees, among the gods who stood guard in the nights, she would fall asleep. The young shepherds would track her down and bring her home.

Reports came about the cloth being measured and cut, but the family visited the city twice and had to return empty-handed both times. The blouses were not yet ready. Being a reputed tailoring shop, they took time to deliver their work.

The stitching, however, would be perfect, they told each other. Meanwhile, the day of the bride's family's visit was nearing. The doctor son was worried. He was afraid that the blouses wouldn't be ready in time. Someone said that since it was a big shop, a word from an influential person would help, and he started working on it.

They told the tailors that they did not need all the blouses immediately: even one would suffice. But the tailors told them that they could deliver only when their time was due and not to worry. They suddenly realized a small tailor could have sewn one single blouse immediately. The doctor found a way out for that too. He discovered a tailor who could deliver a blouse in an hour and received an assurance from him. He was optimistic that he could get a blouse stitched even at the last minute if the reputed tailors let him down.

But did reputed tailors go back on their word? The blouses were delivered a day before the bride's family visited. The entire town turned up at their home to look at the blouses and admire their beauty. 'Adengappa! Look at her luck!' some openly complained. None of them slept at night. Where could she be seated, after taking a bath and wearing a blouse, when the bride's family arrived? What would be the most appropriate place? The ideas poured in.

The next day, when they went to put a blouse on her, she was unconscious and still, her eyes fixed on the sky. The tumour had grown, covering one breast, all the way down to her elbows, stuck to her waist. She couldn't raise her hands. Like a statue of a woman with a winnow in her hand, her hands stopped midway. They would not be raised despite the doctor and his sister-in-law's best efforts. Once again, he was frustrated by her breasts.

'Shit!' he said and took his hands away. The breasts trembled for a moment. Impatient, he shoved at them and left. His sister-in-law was distressed too. There was nothing much she could do. In the distance, they could hear the sound of the bride's car arriving. She bolted the door and ran.

The family was accorded a warm welcome and greetings were exchanged. Beyond the heaps of blouses lying inside, from a corner of the floor carrying the smell of the urine and dung came a thin moaning sound, passing through the silence of the rooms, intruding upon their joyous speech and laughter.

Neelaakka

On a peak summer day, as the sun blazed hot, Neelaakka disappeared. This is what the village remembers her for. Nobody ever found out what happened to her. I was young then, so small that Neelaakka would carry me on her waist. My mother still remembers how I cowered under the bed, frightened by the cries of Neelaakka's frail mother. Like a haunted soul, she wandered the roads with her unkempt hair, beating her chest, screaming 'Neela! Neela!' I was so frightened that I had a bout of fever and became delirious. It took some months for me to recover from a near-death situation.

Not many people talk about Neelaakka now. The villagers decided that she must have eloped with someone, or had a fatal fall in a river or a lake. No man of the village disappeared with her: she might have eloped with an outsider. 'Who would elope with her?' The villagers laughed. It was strange.

I haven't forgotten Neelaakka for all these years. She roams freely in the fields of my childhood. I feel ashamed today when I think of perching on her waist and going about with her. What happened to her, I cannot guess. There is no evidence left to look into today. The thatch-roofed house where Neelaakka and her mother lived is dilapidated now. Occasionally, when I pass the house, I imagine Neelaakka emerging from the broken bricks, a smile spreading over her face as she runs towards me, calling, 'Paiya' – little boy! It feels like it might still happen.

Neelaakka and her mother lived right opposite our house. Life was all about hard work for both of them. I never saw Neelaakka idle. There was no job she couldn't do: from labouring in the fields to working in construction sites, she did everything. She didn't like to stay idle at home. She always created her own opportunities for work.

On her way to work in the mornings, she would come and pinch my cheek, calling me 'Kannu paiya', beloved boy. As soon as she would come into view, with her tightly braided curly hair, I would be ready, showing her my cheek. She knew how to pinch it without inflicting any pain. She always adorned her plait with flowers, even if they weren't jasmine or firecracker flowers. It was a sight to watch her walk till she disappeared, the flowers hanging from her hair.

There was something masculine about her face. Still, I loved taking in the smell of the powder she applied, on the skin she washed with turmeric. The bindi in the middle of her forehead shone bright. She wore her old, faded saris with grace.

Her mother cursed her often. 'It is to dress like this that she runs after work.'

All the children liked Neelaakka, just as I did. She would bring peanuts or fruits and hand them out generously to us. 'Neelaakka, Neelaakka!' they would cry when they got hold of them. Incensed with jealousy, I used to tell them, 'She is my Neelaakka.'

'She's our Neelaakka too,' they would reply.

I would then make a list. 'She lives opposite our house, she pinches my cheek every day, she gives me extras of everything.' Unable to respond, the boys would make faces at me and run off. Filled with pride, I would run after Neelaakka, clasp her hand and walk back home with her.

She was very fond of children. 'What kind of smile is this?' her mother would chide her. 'Spend some time with them – you will know,' Neelaakka would answer. There was a path from the field that led to her home without crossing the village. Yet she always walked through the village.

Her happy demeanour changed totally after a visit from a prospective groom from Aniyur. The groom was also a farm worker. They both took a liking to each other, and the marriage was almost finalized when Neelaakka chanced upon the groom's widowed sister one day on her way back from work. Neelaakka spoke with her, smiling, and the woman had a shock.

'Look at her teeth, they are *stained*!'

The smile on Neelaakka's face faded. It never returned. The voice of the white-clad woman was not an ordinary one. It was as if she was seated on a full-grown palm tree and announcing it to the entire world. She spoke like a spectre that had found a human host. Every face that Neelaakka came across afterwards spoke in the voice of the white-clad woman. But it was laden with sympathy or sadness. It sought to sharpen its sight to find the stained teeth when Neelaakka spoke. Neelaakka couldn't understand why these beings had lost their original voices and looks.

Then, people started speaking of treatments and remedies. After all, only two front teeth had some crescent-shaped stains. They were marks left by the tender fruits of palms that she had tried to bite when she had been a child roaming after the goats. Some said the stains wouldn't go away. Some suggested brushing with powdered brick, which would make them disappear in a month. Neelaakka seemed to like that idea. It sounded better than the others.

No prospective groom turned up to meet Neelaakka after that.

One day, Neelaakka carried an entire brick home on her head from the construction site where she worked. She came home by the path that ran through the fields and not through the village. From that day onwards, she forgot to plait her hair. She forgot the turmeric and face powder. She grew obsessed with her teeth. She would go to the backyard early in the morning and would return well after the sun came up. She kept brushing her teeth with brick powdered with a round stone. She then rushed to work. She even forgot to pinch my cheek before going to work. When I would come out looking for her, she would already be running on the path to the fields, her unkempt hair flying in the wind. There were days she skipped work because she was late.

The brick wore out, but there was no sign of the stains going away. They remained firm on her teeth.

Tears flowed every time she looked in the mirror. 'What are you looking in the mirror and smiling at?' her mother would chide her, but Neelaakka would not pay heed. She would look into both sides of the mirror. Sometimes, she felt that the stain had lost some of its colour. Her face would brighten. But at another angle, the stain appeared stubborn. Her face would turn dull again. The stain appeared to be visible from every angle.

One old lady living at the corner of the street summoned Neelaakka and told her, either out of concern, or to mock her, 'Look Neela, the brick you got might not be of good quality. It should have been properly baked. Find a brick like that and bring it back.'

At the sight of any brick, Neelaakka thought only about whether it was the right one. She looked through the bricks, handled them, inspected them for their quality. Time passed without leaving her any more certain than before. Was this the brick she had been looking for all along? Or was it not the right one?

A full brick would come back, held on her head, after work. For two days, she would use the brick to brush her teeth before giving up on it. *Why did I have to bring one that was not properly baked,* she would ask herself and throw it away. The following day, she would find another brick at the construction site. From inside the structures, she would sift through the bricks like a mad rat digging holes, satisfied with nothing. No one could moderate the speed at which she searched. She seemed possessed with the burning desire to knock down the world with a brick.

One day, she lost her job too. By then, there were

many bricks in front of her house. The house had a large entrance, so nobody raised any questions. She had collected different kinds of bricks. Some were ripe and red, some less ripe and bleached, some with a black dot in the middle. Her anger and speed stopped me and other children from going anywhere near her. We were afraid of her dead white face. She was deformed, like a brass vessel hit by a stone. We were always cautious lest she threw a brick at us.

'Neelaakka, Neelaakka!' I would often blurt out. But she was in a different world even when our paths crossed. I didn't know how to bring her back to our world.

Neelaakka had quit construction work, but not collecting bricks. She travelled tirelessly, far and wide, to find the right brick. She went to every village in the vicinity, looking for the right brick at construction sites. Everybody knew her everywhere: 'brick thief' they would call her. She was troubled by the fact that she couldn't patiently inspect a brick before picking it, but she had no choice either. From morning into the afternoon, she would brush her teeth with the bricks. In the evenings, she would go hunting for more bricks. Late into the nights, you could hear the small sounds of Neelaakka brushing her teeth. I was afraid of waking up to pee and used to call my mother to stand guard. Whenever I went out, I would turn back and catch a glimpse of her figure in the dark. She was bothered neither by us nor by the sounds we made. She was too obsessed with the bricks.

She looked for bricks not just at construction sites. She went looking for them constantly in the fields and carried small pieces of brick back home in her sari. She might even have found some ancient bricks. Sometimes, she jumped for joy after finding one, like she had unearthed a treasure. She would keep them hidden, worried they would be taken from her.

The uneven heaps of bricks in front of her house grew like an anthill, and she sat among them brushing her teeth. Her saliva turned red, and the stains of the red saliva changed the colour of the entrance. Neelaakka's mother screamed at her, complained and wept. But Neelaakka looked lost and sat amid the piles of bricks. The red saliva flowed among the heaps of bricks, like the dirty water that kept flowing when cleaning the house.

In the village which had given her names like 'brick thief' and 'brick-picker', she was now called a lunatic. None of it worried her. She had started living with the bricks. They became her food and water. The relentless brushing left a dent in her index finger. The blood was of the same colour as the brick. Her mother would occasionally step inside the heaps of bricks, and pull her out by her hair.

Neelaakka

She would then make her sit on the porch and step into the house, but by the time she returned, Neelaakka would be back inside the bricks. Far removed from the cries of her mother and the curses aimed at her, Neelaakka hid amidst her bricks.

I have seen her during those moments. They were the only moments in which I saw her fully too. Her body was thin and brick-red – it had shrunk like that of an old woman. She did not know any of us any more. The porch was a world to which she did not belong. She felt alien sitting there. She no longer liked our lands, winds and smells, and found them suffocating. It was the heaps of bricks that gave her solace.

One day, she spontaneously started tearing out bricks from the walls of her house. Her mother first thought it was a hole made by a rat, but realized the truth when the hole widened. She beat Neelaakka hard with a broom. Neelaakka shed not one tear, nor did she let out a word of pain. It was her mother who wept and complained, pointed fingers and hurled abuses.

Finally, she warned Neelaakka, 'Look, I am going to call the truckers and ask them to take these bricks away.'

The only response from Neelaakka was a hard stare.

For some days after that, no one dared to go round that side. Sometimes, her mother stood on the porch and looked into the heap of bricks. She could spot Neelaakka's head, which was constantly shaking. The saliva flowed outside the bricks.

When that day dawned, no one could step on the street, which already lacked proper drains. On that day, saliva mixed with brick flowed through the street. It had a foul smell. The vultures smelt the odour and circled overhead. Enraged with Neelaakka, the village walked towards her place. As they went near, the odour became stronger. A flood of saliva flowed from every corner of the brick hillocks. The crowd started to pelt stones. Neelaakka was not inside.

After looking for her daughter everywhere, her mother started crying, 'Neela! Neela!'

The insects hid themselves away, frightened by her voice. They were brick red in colour, with the ends of their moustaches curled.

Acknowledgements

First and foremost, I owe my gratitude to Perumal Murugan for trusting me to translate these stories. The stories are special in that they are representative of Murugan's oeuvre. He was also readily available to clarify any doubts, however silly or basic. There is no way I could thank him enough.

I thank Kannan, publisher of Kalachuvadu Publications, for his constant support and guidance, with this work and many others.

Working with Supriya Nair for editing the stories was a learning experience. I owe it to her for her keen eye. I am also thankful to Arani Sinha and Devangana Ojha for their help with the stories, for raising important questions and for their gentle prodding.

My discussions about the stories with P. Sainath, with whom I have had the honour of working for the last few years, were again enriching and helpful.

Murali, my husband, was a constant source of support pulling me out of the inertia I tend to slip into and constantly reminding me of the importance of this work.

And finally, to the women and men of Murugan's stories who are perhaps living in some remote village in western Tamil Nadu, wrapped in anonymity, for the lessons they offer. They are lessons for life.

Acknowledgements

First and foremost, I owe my gratitude to Perumal Murugan for trusting me to translate these stories. The stories are special in that they are representative of Murugan's oeuvre. He was also readily available to clarify any doubts, however silly or basic. There is no way I could thank him enough.

I thank Kannan, publisher of Kalachuvadu Publications, for his constant support and guidance, with this work and many others.

Working with Supriya Nair for editing the stories was a learning experience. I owe it to her for her keen eye. I am also thankful to Arani Sinha and Devangana Ojha for their help with the stories, for raising important questions and for their gentle prodding.

My discussions about the stories with P. Sainath, with whom I have had the honour of working for the last few years, were again enriching and helpful.

Murali, my husband, was a constant source of support pulling me out of the inertia I tend to slip into and constantly reminding me of the importance of this work.

And finally, to the women and men of Murugan's stories who are perhaps living in some remote village in western Tamil Nadu, wrapped in anonymity, for the lessons they offer. They are lessons for life.